A MATTER OF TRUST

A MATTER OF TRUST

BARBARA NESBITT

KIDS IN BETWEEN, INC.
409 Arbor Meadow
P.O. Box 1037
Ballwin, MO   63021

DEDICATION
This book was written for those young people who
struggle to find out who they are, and how they
can find happiness.

CHAPTER ONE

Cory stood looking at herself in the mirror. There wasn't much about her face and her shape that she didn't want to change. Her brown hair was too straight and her blue eyes seemed far too narrow to suit her. Cory turned around so that she could look at herself from the side. The long orange scarf that she had pulled through the loops of her white shorts already looked wrinkled. Cory hated the fact that other girls always seemed to look like the teenage girls in the magazines, and no matter what Cory wore, she was sure the clothes didn't fit right. She gave a deep sigh of disgust, feeling cheated at not seeming to have more to offer to the world than a thin body, a dull mind, and stringy hair.

Her staring into the mirror was interrupted by her mother's voice. "Cory, can you come here a minute?" Cory closed her eyes and tried not to think how her mother's voice always seemed angry. The falsely pleasant tone sounded worse when her mother made an effort to appear calm when Cory knew she wanted to scream at her to get in the kitchen. There would be the usual Saturday morning argument over what Cory had missed when she cleaned the kitchen. Fingerprints on the cabinet by the refrigerator. Or it could be the refrigerator itself. Probably the inside, Cory shrugged. She knew she had skipped wiping off the refrigerator shelves because cleaning them just didn't seem important this morning. Mainly, though, it would be the floor. Always there was something about the floor. It wasn't swept properly before it was damp mopped. Chairs weren't moved properly, and somehow her mother found something under the table. There wasn't a Saturday when Margaret Webber didn't find *something* that her daughter had left under the table.

"Coming, Mom." Cory quickly lifted the sides of her hair and sprayed only a small mist of hairspray. She wanted her hair to look natural. Matt liked girls who didn't wear makeup and who didn't appear to have spent any time fussing with their hair. Cory glanced at the giant Mickey Mouse clock that hung over her bed. It was nearly eleven. Matt would be at the shopping mall by noon. Cory threw her brush down. It enraged her that her mother's complaining might make her late and that she'd have to keep Matt waiting.

Matt now was the most important person in Cory's life. Whatever he wanted to do was what Cory wanted to do. At last she felt as if she really belonged to someone. Matt's friends accepted her for who she was. It didn't matter to them that Cory was a nobody at school and that she came from a home where there was no father and only a mother who barely earned enough to support herself and her child. There was a great deal of comfort for Cory in being able to share the fact that Matt and all of his friends also came from homes where there was only one parent.

"Cory, are you planning on coming out of your room or not?" Her mother's voice wasn't as calm now. She was annoyed at Cory's delay because there already were so many things that she had to crowd into a busy Saturday morning. Margaret had little patience with her daughter and the primping that never stopped since she had met Matt.

"I said I'd be there. Why do you always have to yell about everything?" Cory slammed her bedroom door. The closed door was a symbol of the privacy that Cory demanded from her mother. Cory had told her mother that under no circumstances did she want her to go into her room or to touch anything that belonged to her. Margaret had agreed that she would not go into her daughter's room as long as the room was kept clean and presentable. Cory was not sure why the room had to be *presentable*, as her mother said, because no one ever came to the small apartment.

"So what is it I've done wrong this morning, Mom?" Cory folded her arms across her chest as she leaned against the wall and waited for her mother to find whatever fault she was going to find.

Margaret stood looking out the window. For much of her married life Saturday morning had been the first day of an enjoyable weekend with her husband and child. Now she thought back bitterly as she recalled how year after year the marriage began falling apart until she and Daniel shared nothing in common. Their Saturdays became filled with the same type of anger that she and Cory now shared. Ever since the divorce three years ago, Saturday became the day when Margaret struggled to find the time to do all that had

3

to be done before it was time to go to bed on Sunday night.

As Margaret gazed out the window and across at the small apartments that were so like her own dingy living arrangement, she could feel Cory's presence in the kitchen. Turning to face her daughter for the argument that she knew was going to take place she asked, "I assume that you think there is something wrong?"

"I could tell from the tone of your voice. Mom, the only reason you call me into the kitchen on Saturday morning is to gripe about something I have or haven't done. Can we just cut through it all and you tell me what it is that still has two specks of dirt on it? After all, the world might come to an end if a piece of dust got into this crummy place."

Margaret spun around, still trying to keep herself from getting angry at a daughter who knew only how to pout and defy. "All I'm trying to do, Cory, is to teach you that there's a right and wrong way to do things. If you do something halfway, you might as well not do it. You can't go through life not doing what you're supposed to do. If you're cleaning a kitchen, you clean the kitchen and you clean it like it's supposed to be cleaned. You don't..."

Cory hit her fist against the wall. "Please, Mom, I can't stand to listen to that lecture one more time. I want to throw up when you start that stuff about how you're this great big help to me. How you're going to make my life this great and wonderful thing because you'll see to it that I clean a kitchen like it's supposed to be cleaned. Do you

4

have any idea how sick I get of hearing you? I'm an adult, Mom. You treat me like I'm some stupid kindergarten kid."

"Cory, be quiet." Now Margaret's voice sounded more like the angry mother that she was. "Stop telling me what it is I'm trying to do. Your room looks like a pigpen. You're supposed to keep your room clean. Remember that agreement, young lady? Do you?"

Cory hated it when her mother called her young lady. "It is clean."

"It isn't. If clothes are piled on a chair, the room isn't clean."

"A couple of outfits on a chair doesn't make a pigpen. Pigpens are filled with mud, Mom. There isn't any mud in my bedroom."

"You just take everything and twist it around, Cory. All I want you to do is to grow up to be a neat, clean person. And you can begin by mopping this floor again. It's beyond belief that you think you did this floor right."

Cory paced back and forth. "I don't believe you. I honest to God don't believe you. That floor looks perfectly fine to me. You're just not happy unless you're picking on me about nothing. Maybe you want me to get down and lick it clean with my tongue so that it will glow. Maybe I could put wax on it with a toothbrush or something like that." Cory twisted the orange scarf until the threads came loose.

Margaret came to where Cory stood and pulled on her

arm. "Look, Cory, there's jelly on the floor. It's the same jelly that you spilled Tuesday. I left it there after you spilled it because I wanted to see if you'd get it cleaned up on Saturday. You didn't. Hardened jelly on the floor and you think I'm going to accept that. Well, I'm not. Get out the mop and do the floor again."

Cory just stared at her mother. How could her life be so empty and so meaningless that what happened to jelly seemed to be all that mattered to her. Cory's voice shook when she answered her mother. "Mom, I'm going to meet Matt. He's going to be at the mall at noon. I'll do the darn floor when I get back."

"No, Cory. That's not how you run a life. You do what has to be done. Then you play."

Cory's stomach ached from all the arguing. She wanted to punish her mother for ruining one more Saturday. Cory said what she knew would hurt her mother. "You know, Mom, I can see why Dad left you. You're impossible to live with. No one could live with you, Mom. No one, and that includes me as well as Dad."

"You're hateful, Cory. Plain hateful." Her daughter's words stung. Even though it had been three years since Daniel had left his wife and young daughter, Margaret still felt the pain of his asking for a divorce because he said he couldn't live with her anymore. What her daughter said brought the pain to the surface and she had no strength to go on fighting with Cory. "Forget the floor, Cory. I'll do it myself." Margaret bit her lip and tried to keep from crying.

All she had left was Cory and she couldn't seem to get along with her no matter how hard she tried. "I'm tired from working all week, but I still have enough pride to care about what my house looks like. Stepping on sticky jelly is not..." Margaret turned away so that Cory couldn't see her cry. She simply didn't want to say one more word about floors or jelly.

"I'm not sure when I'll be home, Mom. Am I supposed to back at some certain time?" Cory didn't feel particularly good about having won the battle with her mother. She knew she had worn her mother down and there would be no demands about getting back for supper.

Margaret felt as if it were totally pointless to say anything about Matt. She had only met him twice, but she didn't trust him. There was something about him that was too smooth and too arrogant. He had answers for everything. Margaret thought a seventeen-year-old boy should be a little shy, or a little unsure of himself. Matt fired out answers to anything Margaret wanted to know, yet, she knew that most of what he said was untrue. Margaret found it very annoying when he had visited the apartment and walked around touching all her possessions, wanting to know such personal things like why she had a green couch and a peach chair. She told Cory that she thought she could find someone nicer than the bold, young man who showed no respect for an adult.

It didn't matter to Cory what her mother thought of Matt. Ever since Cory had met him, Matt had given her a purpose for living. The things they did together and with his friends made Cory actually feel like she was a person who was at least noticed by someone.

Margaret stared at her daughter. "I don't suppose I even need to ask, but I imagine you're going to waste another day hanging out at the mall all day."

"And what's wrong with that? That's what all the kids do."

"They didn't when I was your age. They read books or did volunteer work. Something useful."

"Yeah." Cory's lip curled in anger. "And you're the perfect example of how a wonderful kid turned out to be this super adult."

"Be back by a little after five if you want to eat." Margaret could not bear to exchange one more harsh word with her daughter. "If you're not back, I'll leave your supper in the oven."

Cory felt relieved. Now no matter what time she came home, it would have to be acceptable because her mother had not given her a time. Her mood brightened to the point that she was able to walk around and give her mother a kiss goodbye. "Forget the floor, Mom. I said I'd do it when I get home. Bye. Have fun today." Cory didn't know why she said that. Her mother never seemed to have fun doing anything. She touched her mother's arm hoping that it would ease the guilt she felt over having hurt her. Then Cory raced out the door.

The mall was crowded as it always was on Saturday

morning. Seeing girls her own age walking in small groups or seeing students from school laughing and talking with their friends no longer bothered Cory the way it used to. Now she had her own set of friends and she no longer felt alone and left out. Cory smiled or waved at those who at least recognized her from school. The smiles and waves were meaningless on Cory's part and on the part of those who were merely being polite. Even if they were kind enough to be polite, they never asked Cory to join them in any sort of activity either at school or away from school. For that Cory blamed her mother. If they hadn't had to move three times in a little over a year, Cory was sure that she would have made friends and have been some part of what took place at school.

Cory held her head up and walked with a self-assurance that she hadn't known in a very long time. In a few minutes she'd be with her friends. What other people her age were doing at the mall wouldn't matter. All the changes in her she believed she owed to Matt. A feeling of excitement passed through Cory as she thought about how grateful she was for the night her mother sent her to the convenience store for milk and a newspaper. Matt was coming out the door as Cory entered the store. He smiled at her and said, "If I had known someone like you was coming along, I wouldn't have made any plans to leave." He turned around and walked back inside the store. As Cory walked over and opened up the dairy case, Matt ran his hand up and down the shelves. "Tell me when to stop and I'll pick out just

9

what you need."

"Pevely milk. A half gallon." Cory didn't know what to make of the tall blond boy whose smile didn't disappear. No boy had ever spoken to her in such a flirtatious way. Cory wished that she could think of something clever to say. Anything that would show him that she was not some dumb, stupid girl who had never been around boys. "We drink a lot of milk at our house."

Matt reached inside the dairy case and took out the milk. "And where is that house where you drink so much milk?" He held onto the half gallon. "Anything else?"

"Just a newspaper." Cory wondered what was going to happen after she paid for the milk and had to leave the store. All the warnings of her mother and the warnings that she had heard in different classes at school came to mind. The boy was a stranger and she had not the slightest idea if he were just a young man who happened to like her or if he meant her harm. Suddenly Cory felt uncomfortable because she couldn't imagine why a nice looking boy would bother talking to her unless he meant her harm. "That's all the help I need. Thanks." Cory stepped up to the counter to wait her turn.

"Hey, listen, that's why I'm here. To help out pretty girls such as yourself. You got a name?" Matt stood much too close.

She couldn't see how his knowing her first name could increase or decrease her chances of being harmed by the stranger who saw fit to talk to her. "Cory."

10

"You must live around here or you wouldn't be walking to the store."

"Yeah. I live pretty close by." Cory felt her legs trembling as she thought of him following her out of the store and then having to go down Folker Street where it always seemed to be dark and deserted. Cory hated that street.

"Mind if I walk along with you?"

"Yes, I do mind. I was capable of getting down here by myself, and I'm just as capable of getting home by myself."

"Oh, no." Matt slapped the palm of his hand against his forehead. "Here I thought by accident the love of my life had walked in the door. Instead you're going to turn out to be one of those snoots who thinks she's too good for me. What a life I lead. To be dealt such a blow when I didn't deserve it." His grin remained as he openly teased her.

"I'm not a snoot. I'm just careful. There are plenty of really weird people around. I think one of them passed me when I came in the door."

Matt made a face at her. "I'm not weird. I'm just a guy who got a look at those beautiful eyes of yours and thought you were worth a try. I am so *sorry*," he stressed his apology, "if I offended you." Matt backed away from the counter and smiled at the clerk. "The last thing I want to do is make a pretty girl angry."

Cory couldn't believe that he was saying she was pretty or that she had beautiful eyes. Except for Keith Andersen, no boy had even noticed her let alone asked her out.

Cory's dad kept telling her not to worry about dates.
"You're still pretty young, Cory. One of these days you're
going to grow up and the guys will go nuts over you.
That's the way it always happens. You can't get any guy to
notice that you're alive. Then the next thing you know,
you turn sixteen and you'll have to hang up on them to get
them off the phone."

It didn't happen that way for Cory. Eight months ago
she had turned sixteen and no boy at school noticed her any
more than the boys did in grade school or in junior high.
Cory knew that she wasn't the prettiest girl in the world,
but she also knew that she wasn't ugly. The thing that
Cory believed about herself that kept anyone, and that
included girls as well as boys, from noticing her was that
Cory saw herself as dull. More than anything Cory wanted
to have some spark to her. Something that would make
other students see that she had some life and that she could
be fun to be around. The spark, though, simply wasn't
there. Cory accepted that she was just alive. Just a student
who walked from class to class and never had anything to
say that might interest anyone. Cory came to believe that
she was just an invisible person that no one bothered with
one way or the other.

Looking back on the night that she decided to take a
chance and let Matt walk her home seemed like the smart-
est thing that she had ever done. On the walk back to the
apartment he did most of the talking. Matt was like the
person Cory dreamed of being. He was funny and never

ran out of things to talk about. Whereas Cory was afraid of new things and new places and meeting new people, Matt saw life as an adventure filled with dares. By the time Cory put the milk in the refrigerator and handed the newspaper to her mother, she felt that her entire life had changed.

Cory only mentioned to her mother that when she went to the store she had met a boy who was about her own age and that he had walked her home. The lecture her mother gave was expected. She talked of the foolishness of allowing a total stranger to pick her up in a store. Her mother's warnings made Cory smile. While Margaret's words about the danger of leaving the store with Matt kept coming out of her mother's mouth, Cory glowed as she thought about Matt's smiling face and heard his happy voice. That he actually asked her out to a movie baffled Cory. It was impossible for her to believe that she deserved to be asked out by a boy as nice looking and as interesting as Matt.

Until Saturday night came and Matt actually rang the bell, Cory doubted that he would really show up. She told her mother several times that even though he had asked her out for a date, she was sure that he hadn't meant it. It made Cory angry that her mother agreed that she might be stood up. Cory thought her mother should have encouragd her to believe in herself. When the doorbell finally rang and Cory threw open the door, she smiled a lovely smile and said, "I don't think my mother believed you were true. I know she thought I invented you."

That Saturday night was the beginning of a whole new world for Cory. There were other dates. There was the first kiss. There was the unreal and wonderful feeling of knowing what it was like to be in love. There were the friends that Matt had who became Cory's friends. Her mother didn't matter, seeing her father didn't matter, and school didn't matter. The only thing that had any importance to Cory was making time pass until it was the hour and the minute when she would see Matt again.

Cory grinned when she looked down the mall and spotted Matt. His blond hair was hanging across his forehead. Lorie, Nicole and Larry were with him. Matt sat on the railing that overlooked the escalator. A security guard was talking to Matt. The guard warned Matt to get off the railing or to get out of the mall. Matt's intentions were to obey the guard, but to do it as slowly as he possibly could. One foot touched the floor and his rear end was barely off the railing. He saw Cory. A beautiful grin spread across his face. "See, Sir," Matt looked at the security guard, "that's my girl. Now if she wanted me off this railing, I'd get off in a second because anything that girl wants, she can have."

"Get off that railing." The guard ignored Matt's attempt to delay and to have his way. "You kids gripe and complain about the way you're treated here, but you all act like fools. You don't care whether you endanger your life or anyone else's. You stupid kid. You could fall off here and knock someone down the escalator."

Matt made an effort to bow to the guard. "Yes, Sir. Yes, Sir. Anything you say, Sir. I sure wouldn't want to kill a whole bunch of people on Saturday morning. I might ruin their Easter or something. Hey, Cory," Matt had removed himself from the railing and wrapped his arm around Cory's waist, "how about I take you to see the Easter bunny. We'll all get our pictures taken with the bunny rabbit. What do you say?"

Lorie broke out laughing. Nicole grabbed Matt's arm. "You're crazy, fellow. Real crazy. Sounds like a great idea. I don't have any pictures of me with Santa Claus. I might as well get one with the Easter bunny."

Cory only smiled and whispered, "Whatever you want to do, darling. Just whatever you want to do." The thought of waiting in line with the little children made Cory blush. She didn't want to be the center of attention, but when she went any place with Matt, they always seemed to end up drawing attention to themselves. Cory looked at Larry. She was sure that he felt as she did. Larry always seemed to be uncomfortable when Matt started his craziness or suggested they do something that Larry knew was going to get them in trouble.

Matt leaned over and kissed Cory on the mouth. "How about it, Cory? Do you want your picture taken with the Easter bunny?"

Cory glanced up after Matt took his mouth away from hers. She saw two girls from school staring at her. It made Cory feel good to know that two of the most popular girls

15

at school had just seen her being kissed by such a nice looking boy. "If that's what everyone wants to do."

"If that's what everyone wants to do." Matt raised his voice and mocked Cory. "Come on, woman. Get an opinion. Get a feeling. Say what you want to do. You got a brain. Use it."

His words made Cory shudder. They sounded like something one of her parents would say. "I just meant that it didn't matter to me what we do."

Matt took Cory's arm and pulled her along. "What *does* matter to you? Near as I can tell it's nothing." Matt and Cory walked ahead of Larry, Nicole and Lorie who were trailing behind waiting to see what Matt had planned for this Saturday morning at the mall. Matt didn't say anything to Cory for a few minutes as they walked past the stores filled with new spring clothes. "So, if it doesn't matter to you, how about we get ourselves a new outfit?" He paused for a minute and waited for his friends to catch up. "Old Matt has decided what we're going to do. A little team work here, please." Matt nodded to each one of them. "We're going to get ourselves a few new things because we're so great we deserve something. In fact we deserve the best. Right?"

Cory's heart raced. This was the thing that she dreaded the most. She couldn't stand it when Matt started talking about their deserving something. That meant that he wanted all of them to shoplift. Only Matt and Nicole found the stealing exciting. Lorie refused to steal anything. Larry

16

and Cory were nervous, but they were more afraid of what Matt would say than they were of getting caught. Having been caught once, Cory feared that the next time she would not be so lucky.

It had been nearly a month since a store detective followed Cory out of the jewelry shop. She placed her hand on Cory's arm and asked her to wait. "You've got something that you didn't pay for. That's stealing." The woman kept her fingers on Cory's arm. Cory looked to the place where Matt and Nicole had been standing talking to the clerk. They had interested the clerk in showing them some watches while Cory slipped a pair of gold earrings into her pocket. Even before the detective had radioed for a security guard, Nicole and Matt had disappeared. Cory felt alone and deserted. The tears started and her face felt flushed. She was too frightened to look up to see if anyone she knew was seeing what was taking place.

Cory gasped out, "I'm going to be sick." Then she ran toward the ladies' room and threw up. For several minutes she could not pull herself up off the floor. From beneath the door of the toilet stall Cory could see the feet of the store detective. No matter how much she wanted those feet to go away, they remained there waiting for Cory to come out. Finally Cory knew she couldn't wait any longer. She stood up and left the stall. She walked to the sink and rinsed her mouth. "I'm sorry." Cory glanced at the detective. "I was just scared." Cory sucked in her breath.

The woman motioned for Cory to follow her. The

17

security guard waited for the two of them. Cory looked back and forth hoping that somehow Matt would come and help her. Then she blurted out the lie. "I've never stolen anything before." She kept repeating the lie again and again. "I wanted to get my mom something for Easter. She's divorced and she sort of...she feels like no one cares about her. I wanted to show her that I care. I didn't have any money. Honestly, Miss, I've never stolen anything in my life." Cory tried to look at the detective in the hope that if she made eye contact, the woman would believe her lie.

The store detective had dealt with too many shoplifters. She was positive the girl was lying about it being the first time that she had stolen anything. The woman was sure that the young man and teenage girl had been a part of the theft, but they had exited the store too quickly to be caught. Despite the fact that Cory was the one who was caught, there was something about the girl that caused her to sympathize with her. The store detective could see that Cory was genuinely terrified and that there would be no purpose in calling an officer from the juvenile bureau to come down and get the girl.

The woman motioned for Cory to sit down. "First, I really don't believe that this is the first time you've stolen anything. Those earrings just went inside your pocket with perfect ease." She wanted to make it clear that she wasn't being fooled. "I think that you were genuinely sick. And you should be. You *ought* to feel terrible when you break the law. Whether I'm right or wrong, I don't know, but I

18

am going to let you off on this one. I want you out of this mall and I don't want you back here. Do you understand?"

Cory felt a great sense of relief. All she wanted to do was to get out of the mall and get home. "Thank you. Thank you very much."

"What did I say?" The detective's voice sounded harsh.

"I'm to get out of the mall and stay out." Cory backed away, thinking about nothing other than getting on the bus and getting home to the safety of her bedroom.

"Well, learn one thing today. You might think you're clever and that you can get away with stealing, but if you keep it up, sooner or later you'll get caught again. I'm giving you this break because maybe you'll learn something. Keep that in mind the next time you're about to let your fingers stick to something that doesn't belong to you. You can end up in the courts and that isn't a pleasant experience for you or your family."

"Yes, ma'am. Can I go now?"

"My suggestion would be to stay away from those two who were in on this. I've seen that guy around these malls. He's a criminal waiting to get caught. Very often you're known by the company you keep if you get my drift. I'll be watching out for you and I don't want you in this mall again." The detective waved her arm at Cory. "Out."

Cory thought about the detective and being on the floor with her head hanging over the toilet. The same fears that she felt on the day when she was caught came flooding back over her as Matt and his friends made their way toward the large department store at the end of the mall. Cory knew that she should protest. She should tell Matt that she wasn't going to steal anything ever again because she was too afraid of getting caught. Instead she let him hold her hand as she listened to him tell them all that they'd go first to the men's sportswear department and get a couple of T-shirts for him and Larry.

They entered the store and moved quickly toward the escalator. Cory was sure that everyone could see and hear her heart beating. She wished for the courage to tell Matt that she couldn't go with him, yet, a part of her knew doing something that caused her fear was better than feeling alone and unwanted.

CHAPTER TWO

Margaret watched the clock. It was already quarter to eleven and Cory still wasn't home. The curfew had been set for ten-thirty on week nights. The deadline for getting home on time had already been ignored three times this week. The last thing Margaret wanted to do was have another confrontation with Cory over being late and being with Matt so much of the time. Margaret glanced at the clock one more time before going to her own room to wait for the sounds of the clicking lock that would tell her Cory was safely home. Margaret dreaded talking to Cory about the need for her to take a part-time job. When the subject had come up earlier in the summer Cory had protested, and all the protests revolved around the fact that if she worked, she wouldn't have enough time to spend with Matt and her friends. Margaret pulled the sheet up under her arms and rolled over. No matter what Cory's mood was in the morning, Margaret knew that the time had come to face the fact that Cory no longer had any choices as to whether or not she worked.

The sun made an effort to find its way through the kitchen window. Margaret sat sipping her coffee and doing what she seemed to spend so much time doing lately: looking at the clock. It was nearly eleven and Cory still wasn't up. In two hours Margaret would have to catch the bus in order to get to work on time, and she was determined that she and Cory would resolve the part-time job issue before one more day had passed. Margaret picked up her

21

coffee cup and took one more big gulp before moving toward Cory's bedroom. For several minutes she stood outside her daughter's room. She couldn't understand why she felt intimidated at the thought of knocking on the door of her child's room. Margaret closed her eyes and grimaced just thinking about Cory's sleepy, annoyed voice answering her. Then there would be the argument. Margaret raised her hand and tapped, thinking how Cory had to hate the arguments worse than she hated them.

"Cory, I have your breakfast on the table. Cory." Margaret rapped harder on the door. "Are you awake?"

Cory turned over and dropped one leg off the side of the bed. "I am now." Cory stared up at her Mickey Mouse clock and wondered why her mother hadn't left for work two hours ago as she always did. "I'll get up and eat breakfast later."

Margaret didn't wait for her daughter's permission to enter the room. She turned the knob and stood in the doorway. "I'd really like for you to get up now, Cory. We need to talk. It's rather important."

"Oh, no." Cory pulled the sheet up over her head. "I hate it when you say that, Mom. We *need* to talk. That means you're going to tell me about something I have to do, should have done, or shouldn't have done. Can't I just get up one morning and not have to hear what's wrong with me?"

"Just come to the kitchen, Cory. I'm going to fix myself some more coffee and get ready for work."

Curiosity made Cory ask as she stretched and put on her robe, "How come you're not at work now?"

"That's one of the things we need to talk about. That and a lot more. Please, Cory. Try to cooperate and listen to reason this morning." Margaret waited a few seconds to make sure that Cory was going to follow her rather than sit back down on the bed or turn on the radio.

The pancakes that Margaret took from the frying pan had dried out. Cory jabbed a fork in them, lifted them up, and then dropped them back on her plate. "Why would you bother, Mom? These are horrible looking. At least you could have waited until I got up and then made the pancakes. These look like they were cooked last night."

"Next time make your own pancakes and you won't have that problem." It annoyed Margaret that she had gone to the trouble at all to fix Cory's breakfast. While Cory sipped on a glass of orange juice, Margaret removed dishes from the shelves and cleaned. It was better to be doing something when she talked to Cory than it was just to sit at the table and look at her daughter's angry staring.

"You asked why I'm still home, Cory. Well, it so happens that I've had my hours cut. I guess I'm among the lucky in that I didn't get laid off completely. Jody lost her job. I don't have a clue as to what she's going to do. She has two little ones to take care of. From now on I'm only going to be working thirty hours a week. That means a big slice of money is going, and Lord knows we don't have any money that we can spare."

Even Cory understood the seriousness of losing ten hours of wages a week. "Mr. Lober didn't give you any warning or anything?"

"He didn't have to. We all knew business wasn't going that great. Jody and I both talked about what would happen if we lost our jobs. If I hadn't started a couple of weeks before Jody, I'd have been the one who would be out of work. We've got to do something, Cory. I think you know what the something is."

Cory flipped her slipper up and down on her foot. "You're going to talk about me getting a job, aren't you?"

"Like I said, Cory, we're running out of choices."

"Well, darn it, ask Dad for more money. He always seems to have plenty for his little son who is just the apple of his eye. If Rory can get any toy he wants, I don't see why Dad's firstborn can't get a few extra dollars a month." Resentment boiled up in Cory just thinking about the two-year-old child who took up so much of her father's time. She never wanted her father to remarry, and she certainly found no pleasure in being the stepsister of the little blond-haired child.

Margaret reached over and touched Cory's hand. She easily understood the jealously her daughter felt. "We've both been replaced, Cory, but that doesn't mean that your father doesn't still care about us. In his own way he does. He's not like a lot of men. At least he tries to send us what he can."

"Sure. He sends what he wants. He doesn't send us

what we need." Cory jerked her hand away from her mother's. It made Cory angry that her mother defended her former husband.

"I might as well tell you that this whole thing is complicated by the fact that your father lost his job two months ago. Maybe that helps to explain why I've kept up this thing about your getting a job. At first I kept thinking he'd find work and he could keep sending us rent money. It hasn't turned out that way. There's even a chance he's going to have to leave this area if he hopes to find work. Things just aren't really good now, Cory."

"My gosh." Cory clunked her glass down on the table. "What's wrong with you grown-ups that you can't keep your jobs? What's going to happen to us kids? It's not like we don't have enough to worry about as it is. Now we have to worry about whether or not we're going to eat or have clothes to wear." Cory stood up to rinse her plate off in the sink. "This is just a great world we live in. So secure and wonderful."

"Cory, it's not like you are some little child being made to go out and sell newspapers on the street. For crying out loud, you're sixteen years old. There are millions of girls your age working after school and on weekends. You make it sound as if some crime has been committed and you're being sent to prison. All I'm asking you to do is take that job at Felder's Drugstore. Three times Mr. Felder has said you could work two nights a week and all day Saturday. He's a nice man and he understands our situation. I think when we've found someone who is willing to help, you ought to take advantage of it."

"Okay, and suppose I take the job. All day Saturday and two nights a week. Great! When am I going to see Matt or Nicole or my friends? Between school and working I'll be exhausted. I'm not even going to feel like having any fun."

Margaret simply could not deal with the complaining or the lack of understanding on Cory's part. "Listen, young lady, I'm telling you straight out." Margaret did what Cory hated more than anything: She stood there and waved her finger in front of Cory's face. "We're in trouble. You're father is out of work and can't get the money to help any of us. I'm down to thirty hours a week, which means no frills around here. Bare necessities. I can't even imagine where you get the nerve to talk about having fun and running around in the malls and hanging out at bus stations and all those stupid things you do with your time. Can't you get it in your head, child, we're talking about whether or not we have enough money to eat and clothe ourselves? Don't you get it, Cory? Life isn't one great, big piece of fun. When you're broke there's not much to laugh at."

"Well, tell me this, Mom," Cory raised her voice as loud as her mother's, "you're supposed to be so smart. You and Dad are the ones who have all this advice on how to raise kids and what I should be doing to make my life all neat and tidy. I can't come in this place without you jumping on my case about what I'm doing wrong and what

I should be doing so that I can grow up to be this wonderful adult who has everything in her life in order. I'm supposed to listen to you? I should follow your advice? Here you and Dad can't even keep jobs. You didn't even save any money in case something bad happened. You're almost forty, Mom, and you don't have any money in the bank. I'd say that's pretty stupid."

Margaret felt like such a failure. She couldn't believe that she had raised a daughter who was filled with so much anger and so little compassion for the situation in which they now found themselves. "Cory, your father and me are not the best educated people in the world. We've always worked, though, and we've always been proud of the fact that we've been able to earn a living. Things are pretty tough out there now. A lot of people are finding themselves out of work and struggling to get by. We happen to be among them now, and believe me, young lady, you're going to join in the struggle. I'm telling you for the last time this is serious. We're not talking about whether you clean the kitchen right or whether you get a better grade in English. We're talking about surviving. I told Mr. Felder you'd be in at two, and believe me, you better be there. This is not an if, and, or but situation. This is a situation where you'll talk to him this afternoon and you'll take whatever work he has to offer and you'll shut up and quit complaining."

Cory waited until her mother was in the bathroom before she allowed herself to cry. She couldn't sort out her

27

feelings. There was anger over knowing that her mother meant what she said and that Cory would have to do what her mother demanded. There was guilt that she had been so hostile toward her mother and a questioning that perhaps her mother was right and she had no compassion for anyone anymore. Feelings of self-pity passed through her mind over the realization that she would never have some of the nice clothes or the luxuries that other girls her age had. In the end Cory just let all her feelings tumble together until she no longer understood or cared what she felt. What comfort she had came from the thought that Matt would somehow be of help.

Cory called Matt to tell him only some of what had happened this morning. To Cory's surprise, he said nothing about being disappointed that she was going to have to take a job and that they'd have so little time together. His only comment on the phone was, "So. That's the way it goes. There's nothing we can do about. I'll be by to get you after you talk to that old man. Maybe he won't hire you." The phone clicked and Cory went to get cleaned up for the interview.

Mr. Felder's sympathies were with Margaret, a longtime customer who often had to charge things because she didn't have the money to pay at the end of the month. "And, of course, Cory, you can get a fifteen-percent discount. I've always given that kind of break to my employees." He stood at the pharmacy counter and straightened bottles of vitamins that didn't need straightening. "It goes without saying that I expect you here on time and I expect you to work the days that I have you scheduled. If there's one thing an employer won't put up with, it's an employee who's not dependable."

"I can be dependable, Mr. Felder. I hardly ever miss any school and I'm never late." Cory tried to act as grown-up and as respectful as she could. Even though she often was rude with her mother, the good manners that Margaret had taught her always showed through when Cory was around other adults.

"I'll be having you work for about two weeks with Bailey. Mason Bailey. I think you'll like him. He's been with me about two years. Started when he was fifteen. His father wants him to work for his company this summer. Sort of get a jump on learning his father's business. I'm telling you ahead of time that Mason will set a pace that you might not be able to follow. That young man is a real hustler." Mr. Felder looked over the rim of his glasses. "He's not one to stand around if you know what I mean. If there's not a customer in here, he's doing something to keep the place clean or putting up inventory. I'm hoping that you can be like him in your work habits. Anybody would hire that boy."

Cory tried not to pout. Mr. Felder annoyed her. She thought he was making too much of an effort to warn her that she had to be an outstanding worker if she even hoped to come close to Mason Bailey. Cory tried to remember who he was because even though she had been in the

29

drugstore many times over the years, she couldn't even imagine what this supposedly-wonderful worker looked like. That thought had no sooner entered her head when a tall, thin and very ordinary-looking redhead boy came up from downstairs.

"You have to be Cory." Mason smiled. His large teeth did nothing to improve his appearance, but his smile was pleasant looking. "Mr. Felder told me he thought you'd be replacing me. I'm Mason Bailey."

Cory stopped herself from saying *So what*. "I'm Cory Webber. Mr. Felder also told me that you'd be training me. Is it hard to learn?" She didn't even care what his answer was.

"Not really. You just run everything past the light on the computer. It adds everything for you. You have to keep busy, though. Mr. Felder expects that. I mean he had this one guy and this other flake-head girl. Neither one of them were worth half of what Mr. Felder paid them. You know the kind I mean. They stood around talking and leaning against the wall. They acted like they'd fall over dead if they did a couple of hours work. You be fair with Mr. Felder and he'll be fair with you. Here," Mason handed Cory a box of toothpaste, "this is what I mean. I didn't have any customers and so I ran down and got the toothpaste because I could see we were getting low. I keep some empty boxes on hand and I put a few of this and that in the box. I mean I keep track of what's needed. I don't just go down and pitch anything in the box."

Cory wondered if she sounded as boring to other people as this young man sounded to her. "I'm not here to work today. I just came in to talk to Mr. Felder. I'm not even sure he's going to hire me."

Mason raised his hand up and smiled again. "It's a foregone conclusion. I heard him talking to your mother. I heard her telling him about her getting cut back. Mr. Felder was real understanding. He all but promised your mother you'd get the job. She seemed like an OK lady." He shrugged. "At least for a mother if you know what I mean."

That this complete stranger knew all about the plight of her family angered Cory. "I really don't think my family is any of your business. As far as I can tell your job is to train me. I don't know that any of the rest of my life has any-thing to do with you."

Mason stacked the toothpaste tubes in rows and pushed them over to the side. "So much for trying to be Mr. Friendly and Mr. Helpful. I assume, then, that I'll see you on Thursday night." Mason turned away, wondering how he first thought the girl was pretty. Her frown was unplea-sant and her voice was threatening and hostile.

Cory waited for Mr. Felder to return and confirm that he had hired her. Mason was correct. She was to begin work on Thursday at five o'clock. Cory sighed in relief in knowing that she'd get to see Matt for at least two hours after school before she had to start the wretched job. She thanked Mr. Felder and assured him that she would be at work promptly at five on Thursday. Without saying goodbye or thanking Mason, Cory hurried out the door so that she would be home by the time Matt was there.

Just seeing him sitting on the grass in front of the apartment made Cory feel excited. Suddenly the thought of working and not being with him saddened her. "Hi." She reached down and ran her hands through his hair. "It was horrible, Matt. Just horrible. This absolute geek works there now. Mason. Who would name their kid Mason?" Cory laughed and flopped down on the grass next to Matt.

He reached over and put his arm around her. "Geeks are everywhere. Everywhere. Everywhere." He picked a dandelion and rubbed it against Cory's chin before he reached over and kissed her. "I miss you already."

"Oh, Matt, what are we going to do? I can't stand the thought of not being with you. Can you imagine how boring it's going to be working with that old man? He doesn't walk. He hobbles around like he's one hundred. The only bright spot is the geek will be gone in two weeks. I couldn't take that job if I had to work with him. He's got this flaming red hair and freckles. He's supposed to be seventeen and he looks like he's about twelve."

"Aw, come on, Cory, let's look at the bright side. I can come down and see you. Sort of hang out there and make sure the customers treat my girl right."

Cory frowned, remembering what Mason had said. "I doubt that. Mr. Felder made it clear that he's hiring me. In fact, that's the last thing he said to me was that he didn't expect my friends to be passing time in the drugstore reading or talking to me. Matt, my mother is real serious about this. I can tell this time. I thought she was going to blow up this morning when she got so angry with me." Cory took Matt's hands and kissed each one of his fingers. "We'll have Saturday night. We'll have a couple hours after school. I didn't even tell you, but I don't have to start until five on Thursday and Friday. Then all day Saturday. That's not too bad, is it?" She so wanted his approval and assurance that her working wouldn't change anything between them.

Matt tried to smile. "Sure it's okay. You know Larry was thinking about getting a job himself. Before you know it, I might even get a job. Not any kind of dumb job, mind you. I'm not working for nothing and I'm not doing anything I don't want to do. If you got to work, you might as well do something that you like. Right."

Cory laughed. "You're asking me? Me who has to stack toothpaste and sell bars of soap to all those old people who creep into that drugstore."

Matt reached down and pulled Cory up. "Come on. Let's walk. I don't feel like going to the mall today." He took her arm and wrapped it around his waist. "You know I might just talk to my old man about working. He's dead set against it. He must have said a hundred times that I'm going to work for the rest of my life and that I should be enjoying myself now instead of worrying about earning a living."

A feeling of envy crept over Cory. She didn't like herself for envying the boy she loved. "It must be nice. My dad doesn't even have a job now and here your dad is telling you to relax and enjoy being young. I don't know how you can enjoy being young when you have to work." She was feeling sorry for herself and she knew it. "Do you think your dad makes a lot of money?"

"What do you mean by a lot of money?"

She shrugged her shoulders. "Heck. I don't know. What do you think is a lot of money, Matt? I know we sure don't have enough money let alone a lot."

"I suppose my dad makes about sixty thousand."

Cory stopped walking and gasped. "What! Sixty thousand! You can't be for real! I didn't think anyone made that much money. Darn it. You could take my mom's salary and multiply it by three and you wouldn't come up with sixty thousand. You can't be for real, Matt. That's so much money. I mean a real lot of money." Cory glanced at Matt, wondering why when he always had so much money he stole so many things. In reality, his situation wasn't like hers. Matt could buy whatever he wanted to buy whereas Cory had discovered there was an advantage to stealing. The act of shoplifting gave her some of the things that she wanted and would never be able to afford. She asked what she often thought about. "If you can get anything you want, Matt, why do you steal?"

He avoided the answer and asked her a question. "Why do you shoplift?"

"That's a stupid question. Just look at the clothes I
have. If I had to depend on my mom for money, I wouldn't
have anything." Cory ran her hand down the new blue
flowered shorts she had on. Her mother believed the new
clothes and jewelry were gifts from Matt. Though she
objected strongly to Cory supposedly taking so much from
the boy whom Margaret couldn't stand, Margaret felt some
sense of relief knowing her daughter now had some of the
things that their own limited budget couldn't afford.

"You didn't answer my question, Matt."

"What's there to say? It's fun. Kind of exciting if you
ask me. Don't you get some...what would you call it?
Excitement in the pit of your stomach. I get that way when
I cheat on tests. It's like you're outsmarting those stupid
teachers." Matt broke out laughing. "Matt Grayson. A-
student. Who'd have thought, huh? My dad thinks I'm a
genius."

Cory lifted up her chin and kissed him on the cheek.
"You are a genius. At least you're my genius."

"You know I was just thinking, Cory, if I get a job I
could start saving all the money I made. My mother isn't
going to want anything from me, and Lord knows my dad
wouldn't care if I made twenty dollars a week or two
thousand. He's not going to ask me for anything. I could
start a nest egg."

"And, Mr. Big Bucks, what would you do with this
fortune?" Everything he said and thought amused and
interested her.

"How does this grab you, love of my life? We could get married when I get out of school next spring." His blue eyes glinted as he smiled at her.

"Married!" Cory was very much aware that she loved Matt, but she never once ever thought that he loved her so much that he'd want to marry her. "I can't believe you're saying that. I had no idea you felt that way. Most guys don't want to get married. It's us girls who are supposed to be dogging you guys." Her stomach felt as if it were in knots from the excitement of what he said.

"I get tired of living at home, too, you know. I think it would be great to have our own apartment. We could do what we want to do. No more of those Saturday mornings with your mother. You could get up and do what you want to do. Do nothing if that's what you want. Doesn't sound bad to me. I doubt that my mother would notice I was gone, and I don't see my dad often enough that it would even matter." Matt put his arms around Cory and hugged her tightly. "Think about how great it would be. We'd never have to be apart. Seven days a week we could be together."

Cory was quickly caught up in what he was saying. With no trouble at all she imagined herself in a clean, bright apartment. Matt would be there sitting on the couch with her watching television. They could hold hands when they ate together. "Would we have kids?" Cory saw herself holding a little baby girl who reached up and touched her cheek in a loving way.

"Not right away for crying out loud. We got to get married first and settled down. Get the hang of being married and have some fun and freedom. Maybe in a couple of years we could have kids."

The sun felt warm and the afternoon breeze made the day perfect. "Matt, you mean everything to me. Just everything. If I spent my life dreaming about the most ideal person in the world for me, I couldn't have thought you up, and here you just walked into my life. Plain old me found someone like you." She wrapped her arms around his neck. "Sometimes it doesn't seem real to me. Like what happened to us is like what happens in the movies or in some of those stories I read in the magazines." Cory twirled around and kissed him. "That horrible job seems like the answer to a prayer now. I might even ask Mr. Felder if I can work longer hours. Believe me, Matt," Cory's hands flew up in the air over the elation she felt, "I'm going to watch every penny. We'll both save. By next summer we'll have all we need to get married."

"I don't want you telling anyone. Not Larry or Nicole and least of all your mom. I don't want anyone trying to talk us out of getting married or anyone getting any ideas about our seeing too much of each other."

"I won't. I won't tell a single soul." Cory stopped talking as her mind again thought about sharing every day of her life with Matt. "Let's go look at furniture." Her voice squealed the words out. "We can think about all the things we want to buy."

"Yeah, and we're going to have to *buy* the stuff. I don't have the talent for picking up couches or stereos at the mall." Her grinned and squeezed her hand.

As they wandered through the stores Matt quickly became bored looking at chairs and kitchen tables. "When the time comes, sweetheart, you get what you want. For now let's go get ourselves some tapes or discs. My dad said he'd get me a new system for my birthday. There's some hot stuff out now. Hey, listen. You know what? Getz Sound has got those great big television screens. They like fill an entire room. That's what we need. We won't even have to go to the movies if we had one of those. We could stay home and cuddle on the couch and watch every sporting event on the tube." Matt pulled at Cory's arm as he moved toward the door of the store.

"You know, another thing I been thinking about is how this job at the drugstore might work out just a lot better than we thought."

"What do you mean?" Cory asked.

"You're going to have some chances there that we need to take advantage of. It's like a break for us."

"You got to be kidding. I'll be lucky to ever get a raise and I'm sure not going to get any promotion. Did you think I was going to get Mr. Felder's job or something?"

"Get with it, Cory. I'm talking about chances because you're handling money. Didn't it ever occur to you how much stuff we can get out of that place without that old man even knowing it? I'll bet you anything he's got radios

38

and watches and all sorts of junk we can sell. All I got to do is come in and get them. It's not like that's going to be some turn-on the way it is when we hit up the stores in the mall, but when you need money, you take it from where you can get it."

Cory couldn't believe what he was saying. "Matt, this is different. It's not like Mr. Felder is some total stranger or something. He's a friend of my mother's. He hired me like a favor to my mom. I can't steal from him."

"Don't get all moral on me, Cory. What difference does it make if you know him or don't know him?"

"It's not the same at all. I don't know any of those people in the stores where I shoplift. Those people don't mean anything to me. Mr. Felder knows who I am and everything. If he caught me I'd..." Cory tried to think what it was she would feel. "I'd be embarrassed and my mom would find out. All kinds of things would happen to me. I'm telling you, Matt, it's just not the same. Stealing from him and stealing from the stores is not the same thing at all. Besides, I don't know anyone who wants to buy stolen watches and radios. That's crazy."

"You're crazy." Matt stared her down. "In thirty minutes I could find you a dozen guys at school who'd buy anything I had to sell."

"Matt, I don't even want to talk about it. This is just not going to happen." The disappointment that she felt toward him showed in Cory's face. "Here we've gone from me being all excited and absolutely totally happy

39

about getting married next summer to me stealing from Mr. Felder." She pulled her hand away from Matt's. "I'm just ticked off at you. That's what I am." Cory quickened her step so that she wouldn't have to walk with him.

Matt let her walk ahead for a few minutes. Then he took long strides to catch up with her. He understood exactly how to talk to Cory to make her see reason. "Okay, sweetheart, I'm sorry. I'm like that geek Mason or whatever his name is, huh?" He put his lips next to Cory's ear and whispered, "I don't want to do anything to get you ticked off at me. You're everything to me. There's nothing in my life that matters more to me. You understand that, Cory. Nothing. No other human being matters to me the way you do."

Cory felt the blood running to her head as he whispered words that were so important for her to hear. "Let's just stop talking about all this stealing and my job. Next Saturday I'll be working all day and we won't have a wonderful day like today. Please."

"You're right." Matt put his arm around her waist and stroked her hair. Matt had no problem waiting for Cory to think the situation through. He would bide his time knowing that once Cory started working at the drugstore it would be much easier to persuade her to do what he wanted. That was one of the joys in having Cory rather than some of the other girls he'd dated. Cory always ended doing what he wanted her to do.

CHAPTER THREE

Dan Webber was carrying his son Rory when Cory rang the bell. He'd told his daughter over and over again not to ring the bell. It was her home, too, he always said and she should just walk in. Marie didn't agree. She didn't consider her stepdaughter a part of her family. Looking at Dan laughing and playing with his small son, it was hard for Marie to imagine that he had ever had such pleasure with the sullen, pouting Cory.

"Hi, kiddo." Dan set his child down and put his arms around Cory. "It's a real pleasant surprise that you came by like this. Sit yourself down, kiddo." Rory scooted over close to Dan, wrapping his arm around his father's leg as if to protect himself from the girl who stood over him.

"He's getting big, Dad." Cory tried to pretend as if she were interested in the child who shared the same father as she. "Is Marie home?" It was always Cory's hope that the woman Cory envied and disliked would not be home.

Dan shook his head and sat down. "She's taken a part-time job. We had to have another breadwinner until I could get back on my feet. These are some rough times." He made an effort to smile but his long period without work had taken away most of his spirit. "You can hope for the breaks, but they don't always drift your way. Well, enough of that. I hear you're working. God," Dan reached over and took Cory's hand, "I can't believe my little kiddo is working. It seems I only blinked my eyes and you went from Rory's size to a grown woman. Makes you wonder where the time went. How's that job going?"

Cory squeezed her hands so that her father wouldn't see them shaking. As she sat there in his small house it was beyond her to understand how she ever could have even thought he might be able to help her. There was nothing particularly nice in the house. Nothing to indicate that he had an extra dollar to give her, let alone the more than one hundred dollars that she needed. She dug her nails into her arm and felt rage at the position that Mason had put her in. All Cory could think was that the gangly redhead was hateful and that he was wrong.

"You never did answer me, Cory. I was wondering how the world of work is treating you. You're probably getting a lot of good experience. Young people need all kinds of experiences so when things turn on you the way they have me, you can always get another job because you know how to do so much. You like working?"

Rory kept interrupting with questions about eating and toys. His babbling and his pulling on her father infuriated Cory. "It's hard to talk with *him*. You know, Dad, sometimes I don't see how people stand kids. It's like Rory never shuts up and he always wants something."

Dan stroked his son's arm as he was sure as young as Rory was, the child understood his older sister didn't like him. "He's a baby, Cory. You did the same thing when you were a kid. You want a soda or something? I think Marie has some of that orange drink that you like. Aren't you the one who likes that orange soda?"

That he didn't even know what it was that she liked enraged Cory. "I expect you know every single thing Rory likes to drink."

Dan lost his patience. It was easy for him to understand why Margaret said she had such a difficult time with Cory. She was filled with unreasonable anger. "Grow up, Cory." Dan bent down and picked up Rory.

"I don't know why I came here, Dad. I really don't. I always think I can count on you and mom and the two of you turn out to be these big flops."

"Thanks, Cory. I really needed to hear that. You know, of course, that I'm feeling just great about myself. Lost my job. Can't feed my family. Worry to death about you and your mother getting along. You're tremendous support coming in here and telling me I'm a flop." Dan stood up and pitched a toy puzzle across the room. "The heck with it all. You have to wonder sometimes why you have kids. You really have to wonder."

The tears fell down Cory's face. She simply hated him for what he had said to her. "Maybe you guys should have thought about having kids before you had them. You get us into the world and then you don't care one darn thing about us."

Rory pulled himself up on the couch and looked from his father to the yelling girl. Then he screamed and ran out of the room. Dan followed the boy, leaving Cory by herself. She left her father's house feeling more alone than she ever had. It was as if she didn't know who to be angry with. Mason was the one who caught her and she was more enraged with him than she was over the fact that Matt was doing nothing to help her. Cory doubled her hands into fists and cried as she walked down the street. No one was doing anything to help her, and if she didn't give Mason the money for the watch that Matt had taken, Mason was going to tell Mr. Felder.

Thinking about that dreadful night made Cory sick to her stomach. It was the third time in a week that Matt had come into the store. No matter how many times she asked him not to come, he ignored her pleas. Mason warned her the first time that she wasn't even done with her training and she was already breaking the rules.

Cory turned on Mason when he told her that if Matt showed up one more time, he was going to tell Mr. Felder. Mason's attitude was impossible for Cory to understand. "What's wrong with you, Mason? What's with this loyalty to Mr. Felder? What about me? I'm just like you. I'm trying to earn a living. We got a lot more in common than you got in common with the owner of this place. And besides, what difference does it make if Matt's here. I'm doing my job. I'm learning what I'm supposed to do. You're leaving. What does any of this matter to you?"

Mason didn't say what he couldn't yet prove. The girl's friend was too slick. He leaned on the counters and wrote down the brand names and prices of the items that were locked inside the glass cases. He was bold enough to approach Mason and ask him to take the watches out of the case. Mason watched the young man who he now labeled as *the sneak*. The way Matt handled the watches was not the way one would handle them if the watches were going to be purchased. Matt was eyeing the watches with the intent of figuring out how to steal them and Mason knew it. Cory and Matt disgusted Mason, and because they did, he was determined to set the trap that would catch them both.

Mason was positive that no stealing would take place until after Cory was done with her training. Even the two of them, Mason reasoned, would not be so stupid as to do anything while he still worked there. That was too risky. Mason surprised himself at the way he was able to control himself during his last few days at the drugstore. He did everything he could to act natural and to be friendly with Cory, saying nothing more about Matt hanging around the drugstore. The only comment Mason ever made to Cory was to say, "I've never had a real girlfriend and I sure don't know much about what it is girls like in guys, but I'd be willing to bet you could do better than that guy."

Cory waited until a customer had left. Then she turned on Mason. "How dare you tell me what I could or couldn't do! You're just not happy unless you're butting into my life. Take a look at yourself. You're a geek, Mason. A real geek and you think you're something special. I get so sick of hearing dad this and mom that and dad tells me this and mom does that. You surely don't think I care one little bit about your stupid family and how that wonderful dad of yours wants you to go to college and be some big businessman with daddy's company." There was some relief in finally telling Mason how she felt at his spending so much of his time talking about his family and what they meant to him. Cory could not stand to hear others talk about their families if the family did some of the normal things that Cory only dreamed about doing with two parents.

Mason's brown eyes widened at the girl's anger. "I'll say one thing for you, Cory. You always give it all up and let it be known just how you feel. If you want to know what you're thinking, all you have to do is ask and you let go with all barrels. For someone as young as you are, you're nothing but a crab."

It infuriated Cory that he walked away before she could tell him about all the things that he did that made her so upset. His loyalty to Mr. Felder and to his family sickened her. He thought school was the greatest place he could be, and except for his wrestling coach, Mason could find no fault with his teachers or what he was learning. Cory remembered thinking how the only things that were important to her were putting high school behind her, getting married, finding a decent job and living with Matt forever.

Those plans seemed far from becoming a possibility after Mason trapped her and Matt. Mason's plans worked just as he knew they would. On his last night Mason inventoried all the watches before Cory came in. He had written down the brand names and the prices. Then he took foot powder and lightly dusted it along the glass cases that contained the watches. If one were missing, the outline of a watch case would show up clearly along the glass. Cory, who never bothered to dust a thing, would hardly notice that the shelves were not sparkling clean the way Mason usually kept them. Just before Cory was due in at five, Mason did a printout from the cash register. He knew exactly what had been sold all day. If when he came in early in the morning, any watch was missing and there was nothing on the tape to show it had been sold, he'd do what he had intended to do for the last week: He'd accuse them of taking the watch and make them prove that they hadn't taken it.

When the elderly owner showed up to open the store he was surprised to see Mason already there. "What's the matter, son, you forget you don't work here anymore?" Mr. Felder smiled at the young man whom he liked so much.

"No, Sir." Mason grinned back even though he felt very sad for what the girl had done to him. "I just had a few things to attend to. I wanted to run a tape and make sure that Cory had everything straight. After all, last night was her first night by herself. As I recall, that can be a little unsettling."

Mr. Felder put on his white pharmacy coat. "She seems to be working out. Nothing to compare to you, but not too bad. Or am I just getting old and don't expect too much anymore?" He looked to Mason for an answer.

"There are a few problems, but I think she might work out okay." Mason hated himself for lying, but he'd rather lie to Mr. Felder than to tell him that the girl he had trusted was stealing from him. Mason had already seen that no watch was on last night's printout from the cash register. The spot where the case for the one hundred and seventy-five dollar watch had been was as Mason knew it would be. It was clear of the foot powder that he had sprinkled around the case. Mason folded up the receipt, shaking his head at the stupidity of the two of them for what they had done.

At exactly five-fifteen Mason entered the drugstore. It would be a good time to talk to Cory. The store was seldom very busy at that time as the older people who shopped at the drugstore had taken care of their errands for the day and were home fixing dinner. Cory looked up when she saw Mason standing right next to the pharmacy counter.

"What's the matter? You don't think I can run this precious store without you." Cory pulled a cardboard box toward her. "See. The whole box is filled with different kinds of bubblebath. It's just like how you told me to do. I'm not stupid you know."

He didn't agree with her assessment of herself. "I think you are."

"Will you just get out of here? You quit so you can go be a trainee for daddy. Get off my case and let me do my job."

Mason saw no reason to put off saying what he had to say. The girl simply was not likeable, and he didn't care whether she cried or ran out the door, he was going to

48

confront her. "You and your own geek are thieves. Stinking, rotten thieves."

Before he said another word, Cory understood that he knew and his knowing terrified her. She took the defensive, hoping that he meant to do nothing more than accuse her. "Listen, Mason, you don't know anything about me. You don't know what I am and you sure have no right to be calling Matt anything."

He reached in his pocket and took out the cash register tape. "There's not a watch on here, but there's one missing. You low, no-goods took it. Honest to God I can't believe that the two of you could be so scummy. Old Mr. Felder barely makes a living out of this place and then you turn around and do him that way. You're not even human. Not even like normal kids. What the hell is wrong with you?"

Cory's hands trembled. She felt as she did the day the store detective had stopped her after she had stolen the earrings. "Get out of here and leave me alone. Get out!" Cory raised her voice. Tears fell down her cheeks.

"I don't want you working here anymore, Cory. You don't deserve a nice job like this one. You don't deserve anything. In fact, you're going to get that watch back or you're going to pay the full price. Not the discount store price, but the full price. Just like any other customer. You wanted a watch and you took a watch, and you're going to pay for it. What you did is a felony. You can be sent to a reform school for that. That's what they ought to do with

49

you, anyhow."

"You're not going to tell on me." Cory defied him. "You'd worry to death what that old Mr. Felder would think. You sure wouldn't want to crush him with disappointment, now would you?" She hoped against hope that Mason's concern for Mr. Felder's feelings would be stronger than his desire to inform on her.

"He'll get over it, but your mother probably won't. You can imagine what she's going to think when she finds out her daughter is a thief." Mason smashed his fist against the counter. "Good God. I can't even imagine what would go through the minds of my parents if they found out I was this rotten thief. Cory, think about it. Think what you've done to hurt your parents and all for that no-good guy that can't do anything but hang out and smile. You can't have a mind that you use. You just couldn't or you wouldn't be in this mess."

Cory visualized her mother's face when she found out about the stealing. It would be angry. It would be hurt. It would be disgusted. Suddenly Cory believed that her only hope was to win over Mason and make him understand that she was sorry. "Please, Mason. I didn't mean to give Matt the watch. He needed the money. He wanted to buy something for his dad and he didn't have the money. He loves his dad just like you love yours. Give us this break. Just this once. I promise I won't ever take anything ever again. Please, Mason. I'm begging you. I need this job. My mom hardly makes enough to get by. My dad's out of work and he's got this cute little two-year-old kid to take care of. You should see him. He's darling. And dad's got this great wife and he needs to help her. Everyone is going to die if they find out what I've done. I want to die myself."

Mason understood so little about girls, yet, he knew Cory was just saying words that didn't mean anything to her. Too often he'd heard her talking about how she really felt. She resented that her mother and father didn't take better care of her. She hated her stepmother and was jealous of the child she now tried to describe in loving terms. The only truth to any of what she said was the fact her father was out of work and her mother didn't earn much money.

"I'm going to tell you something, Cory, you're a dumb thief and a bad actress. You're not pulling one over on me. I got you figured out. You got those tears running down your face trying to make me all sorry for you. The stupid thing about this is that I do feel sorry for you, but not for the reasons you think. I feel sorry for you because you don't know how lucky you are. You got two parents who care about you. They just don't happen to be rich and they happen to be having some problems with getting good jobs. But you should have heard your mother talking about you. Before I even met you I thought you had to be about the best and most wonderful person in the world. Cory's sweet. Cory's responsible. Cory's the best thing that ever happened to me and her father. Mr. Felder was about to cry the way your mother talked about you.

"I about fell over when you showed up. Your mouth looked like it had been tied in a knot from snarling so much. You're mad about everything, Cory. Mad at life. And I don't care. All I care about is that you did a dishonest thing and you're probably a rotten person. Here's the deal and this is the way it's going to be. I'd prefer if I didn't have to hurt your mother, and if I didn't have to hurt Mr. Felder. What I'd really have preferred is if you had never come to work here in the first place."

"You won't help me?" Cory sniffed back tears as she realized that nothing she said had affected Mason.

"I don't suppose you understand this, Cory, but I am helping you. You did something wrong. When you do something wrong you have to pay for the mistake one way or the other. You have the money or the watch by next Friday. If you do, I'll at least know you made the effort to pay back what you owe. If you don't have either the money or the watch, I'm telling Mr. Felder. If he doesn't want to do anything about it, then I'm telling the police."

Cory picked up the cardboard box that lay next to her hand. She struck Mason again and again with it. "You vicious, nasty, horrible person. All you want to do is punish me. You don't want any justice. You don't know anything about being fair. You just want me punished because I said terrible things to you." Cory dropped the box and cupped her hands around her face. "You're not even fair. Not fair at all."

"Maybe you're still too young to know this, Cory, but if something is right, it's fair. See you on Friday."

No matter what she did for the rest of the evening and no matter how busy the store was, Cory could not concentrate. Again and again she tried to reach Matt on the phone. The urgency of her voice even alarmed Matt's mother who offered to get in the car and go look for him. On the one night that Cory needed him by her side, Matt failed to show up at the drugstore. At ten o'clock Cory turned the lights out in the store and set the alarm. When she first went outside to wait for Matt it was only misting. By the time he showed up at ten thirty, puddles were forming in the streets from the heavy downpour.

Matt jumped out of Nicole's car and took Cory's arm. Cory quickly whispered before getting into the car. "We have to talk. Mason knows. We're in trouble, Matt. Very deep trouble." Cory slipped in the front seat, sitting between Matt and Nicole. "Hi, Nickie."

"You look like a wet rat." Nicole patted Cory on the head. "Another great night. I think I can get used to my brother being in the army. I really like having his car like this all the time." Nicole pulled away from the curb. "You don't know what freedom is, Cory, until you've had the joy of owning a car."

"You don't own the car, Nicole," Matt reminded her.

"So add to my misery by keeping track of my life for me." Nicole broke off a piece from the candy bar that she had on the seat. "I can't understand why you don't get a

53

car, Matt. You don't even seem to mind walking."

"I do, too. I'm not riding in any junk car. Until my dad gets me a new one, I don't want any. He starts talking that, 'Now, son, let's you and me take a look at some used cars.' Used cars. Bull. If he can get himself a new car, he can get me one. If I start settling for something that's put together with airplane glue, he'll start believing he got me a car when he bought me a heap."

Cory's hands shook and she felt as if she were going to be sick to her stomach. The only thing that interested her was telling Matt what had happened so that he could do something to solve the situation. She turned to him and said in a low voice, "Matt, we really have to talk. Really. It's so important that we talk. I've got something to tell you."

"We've only got *one* secret from Nicole, and you know what that is, sweetheart." He kissed Cory on the forehead. Matt enjoyed teasing her about their private decision to get married. "Other than that, Nicole can know what I know."

He had never said anything to indicate that anyone other than the two of them knew about his plans to steal from the drugstore. Cory was afraid to say anything for fear that Nicole might not know and her finding out would make Matt angry. Cory leaned over so that her mouth was next to Matt's ear. "It's about the drugstore. About what happened last night. About the wa.." Cory closed her eyes and tried to make the knots in her stomach go away.

"Nicole knows, sweetie." Matt laughed. "It's like a

coincidence or something. Nicole knew I had the watch and she bought it off me, she gave it to..." Matt turned to look at Nicole. "Who'd you say you gave it to?"

Nicole half sang out his name. "Z-I-N-G-L-Y. Zingly my love. I'm crazy about him. I never saw anyone look better in a watch."

"You're crazy, Nicole. You just met that guy last week."

"So. Is there some kind of law that says you have to know someone forever in order to fall in love?"

"Stop it!" Cory leaned forward and hit her fist against the dashboard. "We have to get the watch back or Mason is going to tell on me. He knows we took it. He's going to tell on us, Matt. He's going to tell Mr. Felder." Cory was talking very quickly and hitting her fist as her voice became louder and louder. "My mother is going to know. My stepmother will find out and tell my dad that she was right about me being a horrible kid. We got to get the watch back."

"Cory! Cory!" Matt took her shoulders and shook her. "You're acting screwy. That guy isn't going to tell anyone. I'll bet you whatever you want to bet. He's just running his mouth. If he was going to tell, he'd have told. Besides, he doesn't even have any proof."

Cory dug her fingers into Matt's arm. "He does. He knows the watch is gone and that it wasn't rung up."

"He can't prove we took it. He can't prove anything. You don't have a crime unless you got proof. Right,

Nicole?"

"Don't get me into this. I just paid you thirty bucks and gave Mr. Rod Zingly a beautiful watch. That's all I want to know about any of this."

"Mr. Felder will believe him. What reason would Mason have to lie? Besides, it is the truth. You did make me give you the watch."

"Hey, wait a minute, Cory. I didn't make you do anything. Now listen to this, Nicole. I want a witness in case Cory goes all nuts on me. All I said was that it would be real easy to open the case, slip out the watch, and I could be on my way. Cory had the key to that case. I didn't twist her arm or anything to make her do it."

"I don't think you're as smart as you think you are, Matt old boy." Nicole turned the corner and pulled into the parking lot of the restaurant. "All this excitement is making me hungry. You see, Matt, you, I think, are the receiver of stolen property. That Jeff I used to date got nailed for that. The police didn't want to hear how he didn't break into the building and haul those car parts outside. All they wanted to know was that Jeff was sitting there while his friends were steady loading car parts into Jeff's car. That's receiving stolen property. Jeff got in a whole bunch of trouble."

"So who's the thief, then, Nicole?" Matt opened up the car door and took Cory's arm. "I'm hungry, too. If Cory took the watch and put it on the counter, what is it I'm supposed to have stole? I'm just this innocent guy coming into a drugstore and this clerk hands me a watch."

Cory leaned against the car. Tears raced down her cheeks. "I feel like I'm losing my mind. I'm telling you about this horrible thing that has happened. I'm telling you how I have to get the watch back or how I got to give Mason the money to put in the cash register. You're supposed to be my friend, Nicole. How come you aren't rushing to get the watch back? You, Matt, you say you love me and you're trying to figure out how you can worm out of this and make me look like a thief. What's wrong with you two?" Cory raised her fists and beat against Matt's chest. "You don't even understand the meaning of love."

Matt looked at Cory. He suddenly felt very sad for her. She looked so frightened and bedraggled. "Okay. Okay, sweetheart. Calm down. So we're a disappointment. Come on." He put his arms around her and winked at Nicole. "Matt's here for you. Matt's going to take care of you and everything will be okay. How about the watch, Nicole? Can you get it back?"

"I wouldn't even try. What's the Zingly guy going to think about me waltzing up to him and giving him that nice timepiece and then showing up tomorrow and wanting it back. You don't do things like that."

"Let's just get the money, Matt. Get the money from your dad." Cory held onto Matt's shirt as she pleaded. "That's all we have to do is ask your dad. Think up a lie, Matt. You're super good at thinking up lies." Cory

57

screamed at him.

"Back in the car." Matt pulled on Cory. "You're making a big scene out here." Matt moved over close to Cory. He felt he had to calm her down. "I'm not asking my dad for anything, Cory. Nicole really hit a sore point about him tonight. This whole car thing has me really bent out of shape. He *knows* I want a new car and..."

"I don't want to hear about cars! I want to hear what you two are going to do to help me."

"Cory," Matt scooted up against the door and away from Cory. "You're just acting hysterical over nothing. That Mason isn't going to say or do anything. He's got you so scared that you're ready to believe anything. For crying out loud. He's a teenager just like us. He's not going to turn in one of his own kind to that stupid old man."

Cory had no more energy with which to fight or argue. She tried to lift her arm and she couldn't move it to wipe away the tears coming down her face. "Then your answer is to do nothing for me."

Matt moaned. "There's no reason to do anything now. You said we got until Friday. Let's wait and see what he does on Friday. If it looks like he's going to go nuts and run his mouth, then we got time. We'll do some bargaining and ask him for the weekend. I promise you, Cory, if I think he's really going to tell on you, I'll talk him out of it and buy us some time until Monday. Just don't make me ask my dad. I don't want to go begging to him for anything."

Cory wrapped her arms around her waist. She couldn't stand the thought of Matt touching her. "I just want to go home. I want to be in my own room."

Nicole looked surprised. "I thought we were going to get something to eat."

"Please, Nicole," Cory pleaded. "If our friendship means anything, just take me home."

Matt got out of the car and walked with Cory to the entrance of the apartment. "I am really sorry about all this tonight, Cory. Nothing is going to look as bad in the morning. You take Sammy in your arms and cuddle him and tell him your troubles." Matt reminded Cory of the teddy bear he had stolen for her. "Sammy will understand just like I understand."

Cory shook her head. "You don't understand, Matt. You don't understand anything. You're just like my mom and dad. I need you and you aren't there. There's nothing special about you. Nothing special at all." Cory put her key in the lock.

"So what about Saturday night? Are we going to see each other after work?" There weren't many people who made Matt feel guilty. Cory came the closest. "Not, of course, if you're going to be like this. I can't take this kind of stuff. You're getting through to me."

Cory bent her head so that she didn't have to look at him and ran quickly into the apartment. She slipped under the sheet, ignoring her mother's voice. All Cory wanted to do was fall asleep and find some sort of peace in dreaming that none of this happened. In the morning she sat up startled. She couldn't believe that she had slept in spite of all her fears. Cory ran her hand up and down her arm and thought about whether or not she should tell her mother the truth. No matter how many times she imagined her mother's reaction, it was always painful and always something that Cory chose not to face. Telling her father seemed easier until the day when she confronted him. Looking at how little he had, and resenting him, his wife and Rory, Cory ultimately chose to anger him rather than to ask for his help.

During the week Matt had called her only once. Several times she picked up the phone with the intention of pleading with him for his help. Before she had dialed his number, she hung up rather than deal with his disgust. On Thursday she called Nicole to ask her one more time to try to get the watch back. Nicole said only that she could not deal with the humiliation of asking Rod Zingly to give her back the watch. "Forget about this guy Mason telling on you. He's not going to do it. You'll see, Cory. Trust me."

On Friday Mason was waiting at the drugstore when Cory arrived for work. Mason stared at her. Cory's face was pale and it looked as if she had lost weight in just one week. He fought the urge to feel sorry for her, again reminding himself that she had caused her own problems and in all likelihood, had done nothing to solve them in the last seven days. "So what's the story?" Mason followed Cory inside.

The two of them waited for Mr. Felder to busy himself with the three customers waiting for prescriptions. Cory walked to the magazine rack and attempted to look occupied while she waited to see what Mason was going to say. When it was obvious that he was waiting for Cory to tell him what she had decided to do, Cory finally spoke up. "It's true that I gave the watch to Matt. He asked me to do that and I was stupid to do it. He sold it to my friend Nicole. She gave it to this clown at school. I don't have the watch or the money, Mason. And that's the truth. I'm sort of stuck. That's really the truth. This isn't any lie I'm making up."

"And Wonder Boy? What about his coming through for you?"

"No one came through for me, and that's the way it is." Cory felt such pity for herself as she stood facing Mason. She had never known such isolation and such loneliness. "Not Matt. Not Nicole. Not my parents. No one. Maybe I don't deserve any help."

"Maybe you don't." The urge to fight feeling sorry for her welled up in him again. He still couldn't trust her, though. Mason somehow believed she was tricking him and that if he gave in, she would end up laughing at him or not respecting him. "I'm still going to tell Mr. Felder, Cory. He doesn't deserve to have someone like you working here. Your friend could step right back into your life and you could do it again."

"It doesn't matter anymore, Mason. I don't even care

what happens to me."

"If you don't care, who does?"

"I don't care about that, either. I don't even care whether or not anyone cares. I just want all of this to be over."

"It's going to be." Mason didn't want to spend one more minute talking to her because he knew he was going to give in and let her get away with the theft. When the last customer walked out the door, Mason stepped up behind the pharmacy counter. Cory knew they were talking but she didn't know what they were saying. Suddenly Mason walked quickly out the door, leaving Mr. Felder standing alone. It was several minutes before Mr. Felder called to Cory.

Mr. Felder had no trouble looking directly into Cory's eyes. He was not a man to avoid unpleasantries. "This is a very grave thing that you've done, Cory. If you wanted a watch, you should have told me. I could have arranged a discount, and I could have arranged for you to give me a little each week, or even each month, out of your paycheck. Even though Mason spoke up in your behalf and he gave me the money that you gave him, I don't feel I can trust you. Do you understand?"

Cory looked baffled. She had no idea what Mr. Felder was talking about. "No, Mr. Felder. I have no idea what Mason told you."

"He said that you really wanted a watch and that you took it without paying for it. That should never have happened. Employees just don't do that sort of thing. Never. He also gave me this and said that you'd pay me the rest later." Mr. Felder pointed to the fifty dollars that lay on the counter. "I appreciate your effort to reimburse me. I think the fact that you tried to pay back some of the money shows that at least you have a conscience. That will work in your favor throughout life. It would have been better if you had the courage to have faced me yourself instead of having Mason do it." Mr. Felder pointed his finger at Cory and shook his head. "That was wrong of you. I'm also going to tell you that Mason pleaded your case for you, but the whole thing is just too disagreeable to me. Once a trust is broken, the damage is done.

"If there were a long history of trust, perhaps I'd be more understanding. There isn't that, Cory. You were just a young lady in need of a job. I gave you that job out of respect for your mother who has been coming in here for years. I'm not obligated to you, and I can't honor Mason's request for me to give you another chance."

Cory dropped her chin and looked away from Mr. Felder. "I'm sorry that Mason asked you to keep me on. I really don't deserve to work here." Her breath was coming in quick gasps. "Are you going to tell my mother?"

"Maybe you've seen the error of your ways, Cory. My telling your mother isn't going to undo your having taken the watch. All it would do is hurt her. It's not my purpose to hurt anyone. If your mother asks when she comes in here, I'll simply say it didn't work out. I won't lie for you.

What you tell her is your own business. I'm not even sure what I'd say if she asked me why it didn't work out. I was never good at lying and I gave up on it at a very early age. My suggestion would be that you do the same." Mr. Felder turned away from her.

"I'll see that you get the rest of the money. I'll get another job. I promise I'll pay you back."

"I wouldn't expect otherwise." Mr. Felder extended his hand to her. "I wish you the best of luck and hope that you've learned your lesson."

Cory could not bring herself to touch the old man's hand. "Yes. I believe I have." Cory raced out the door. As she crossed the street and headed for home she didn't notice that Mason stood on the corner and watched her leave the store.

CHAPTER FOUR

At first Margaret was baffled that Cory had lost her job. Something inside her told Margaret that if she continued to ask questions, she would find out something that she didn't want to know about her daughter. That Matt was a part of what happened was not doubted for a minute by Margaret. The simplest thing to do was to urge Cory to get another job.

The job that Cory took at the Dollar Store paid less than she had earned at Mr. Felder's and the hours were much longer. Now, though, there was no need to have the extra time away from school or work because she had no desire to see those whom she thought were her friends. The love that she had for Matt was wiped out by a sense of betrayal. Instead of feeling joy, Cory felt only sadness. Moving through the halls at school once again became a lonely existence. The trips to the mall came to an end because she couldn't bare to be by herself when everyone else seemed to be with friends. When she wasn't at school, she was at work or she slept. Her bedroom became a haven to which she could retreat to cry or to sleep.

The report from the counselor at school worried Cory's mother. Cory was no longer doing passing work in any of her classes. Study halls were used by Cory to sleep. It bothered Margaret that even at school Cory isolated herself from everyone, not appearing to hear or see anything in the world around her. The counselor suggested that Cory seek help by meeting with a group of other troubled youngsters.

The suggestion made Cory cry and withdraw even more from Margaret and school. Day after day Margaret left for work knowing that Cory was not getting out of bed and had no intention of going to school. Margaret found it astounding that she longed for the days when Cory yelled or acted out her defiance. That type of behavior at least showed that Cory had spunk and that she was feeling some emotion. As it was, Margaret believed there was no life left in Cory.

On Saturday morning Margaret rose extra early to do the chores that Cory usually did. She felt remorse at having to say anything to Cory let alone arguing with her as she had done so many Saturdays in the past. She'd watch her daughter pretending to eat food, but most remained on the plate. Then Cory would rise and return to her room to sleep or look at magazines.

The call that came from the juvenile authorities stunned Margaret. By the time Margaret arrived at the large, gray building near the downtown area she was no longer surprised. The way things had been going with Cory made Margaret realize that something was going to happen with Cory. Because of Cory's behavior, Margaret believed a call would have come from school or from where Cory worked to say that some tragedy had occurred. Somehow Margaret understood that Cory could not get better until she had gone down as far as she could go.

Dave Marlowski was the officer who came to speak to Margaret. "I'm sorry about this. I don't know of any parent who wants to do this."

Margaret held out a limp hand. "How long has she been here?"

"We notified you right away." He motioned for Margaret to follow him into his office. "The parents are always called immediately. Do you want a cup of coffee or a soda?"

Margaret shook her head. She looked around at the tan walls that were almost devoid of anything except what appeared to be a few pictures of important police officers. "Can I see my daughter?"

"Of course," Dave nodded. "Officer Washington has gone downstairs to get her." He poured himself a cup of coffee. "I suppose you realize that your daughter is terribly depressed. In fact, I've seen enough of these kids to know that she set herself up to get caught stealing. I think her message is that she needs some help. She doesn't seem to care right now what happens to her. That blank look. Most of these kids come in here with a snarl on their faces. Defiant. A lot of them come in here scared. They are so nervous they have to use the john ten times in ten minutes. Cory was bought in here with the same feelings and emotions as a chair. All she said was that she stole the stuff. She didn't even say that she deserved to get caught and brought in here. I worry more about the quiet ones than I do about the ones who come in here screaming and crying or wanting to throw the furniture around. Depressed kids bother the hell out of me."

Margaret stood up when she heard the door in back of

her open. She put her hand to her mouth in surprise. Cory's clothes looked disheveled and her hair had not been combed. The worst was the empty look that she had in her eyes. "Cory, darling." Margaret went to her daughter and put her arms around her. "I'm sorry, Cory. I'm sorry this happened."

Cory didn't move her hands from her side. "I just took the clothes and jewelry, Mom. They caught me going out of the store with them. I did do it. I steal, Mom. I've stolen all kinds of things over the last few months."

"You two sit down." Dave pulled out a chair for Cory. "Sit next to your mother, Cory. We're going to do some talking."

Cory sat down in the chair. She stretched her legs out in front of her and slid her back low in the seat. Her eyes were shaded with her hand and her voice was barely audible when she answered the juvenile officer's question. "No. I don't know why I stole the things."

"Did you want to get caught, Cory?" He asked as he sipped on the coffee.

"I don't know."

"I think you did. You made no attempt to hide anything. You weren't working with anyone else. You had no plan. You just put the things in a bag and very openly walked out the door. It's like you wanted to make sure someone saw you take the jewelry. You're too smart to do such stupid things. You know, Cory, my job isn't just to see that young lawbreakers make their way into the court and get punished for what they've done. A large part of my job is to find out why they do the things they did and then figure out how the courts can help them. I want to help you. Your mother wants to help you. The help is there, but you have to want to help yourself."

Cory dropped her hand and leaned her head back against the chair. "I don't care what happens." The tone of her voice didn't change. Her answers were almost whispered. "Nothing matters. Don't you understand that?"

"Not today, Cory, but maybe tomorrow things will matter. That's the trouble with getting in trouble. You can get in trouble when nothing seems to matter. By the time that you care that it matters, you're already in the trouble. I spend a lot of my time trying to get kids to see that things do matter. Somehow I'd like to get you to see that you broke the law. People break laws for reasons. They hate the law. They think the law wasn't meant for them. They want to get back at someone so they do something that causes somebody some trouble. There are all sorts of reasons for breaking laws.

"My own gut feeling about you, Cory, is that you planned to get caught breaking the law. Once you broke the law and got caught, you figured someone would enter the picture and do something about it. Maybe you want your parents to notice you, and if you end up at juvenile hall, your parents surely are going to notice you. Maybe you know in your heart that you need help and the only way you're going to get help is to do something pretty bad.

Then the help will come pouring out of the walls. You have to give me information, Cory. Lead me to the reason that you stole with the intention of getting caught."

Cory heard most of what he said. Because he was an authority figure, she felt some need to answer him because she had been raised to respect teachers, police and other adults. She had no answer to give him. She didn't know herself why she took bags from the Dollar Store, walked down the street to a clothing shop and deliberately began putting blouses and earrings in the bags. She never looked around to see if anyone were watching her. Her only intention was to fill the bags and walk out the door. When the clerk stopped her and called the police, Cory expressed nothing. There were no lies and no explanations. As she listened to the clerk tell the police officer about the incident, Cory merely nodded when the officer asked her if what the clerk said were true.

"Cory." Margaret leaned forward and took her daughter's hand. "What Mr. Marlowski says is exactly right. We both want to help you. I can't even understand this. I mean what you did. I only know that I love you, Cory. I can't stand to see you going around like this day after day. Does it have to do with Matt?" Margaret was sure that Cory had broken up with him and the pain of that breakup was what had set the depression in motion. She turned to Dave when Cory did not answer. "Matt was very important to Cory. Something happened to that relationship. And," Margaret added, "Cory lost her job. Nothing has gone right for her lately." Margaret rubbed her hand back and forth across Cory's hand.

"Are we on the right track, Cory? Are you hurting over this guy? Maybe you wanted to do something that would get his attention?" Dave looked directly at Cory as he spoke.

Cory wished that she could feel enough pain so that she could cry. She couldn't feel anything but numbness. "Just leave me alone. Both of you leave me alone. Whatever punishment I got coming, just give it to me and then leave me alone."

Dave stood up and moved himself so that he was right in front of Cory's chair. "It doesn't always work that way, Cory. When you're an adult you can let it fly like that. If adults want to mess up their lives, they can make that choice. When you're a teenager, though, other adults can get into your life and make decisions for you. We're trying to head troubles off at the pass because we think we know what's best for you."

The juvenile officer looked more at Margaret than at Cory as he continued talking to the girl. "I don't think we have any hardened criminal here. Not much good is going to come of recommending that Cory be sent to a detention center. Being away from you and her father, Mrs. Webber, is not going to serve much purpose at this point. Cory, what you need is to get yourself in counseling. As I under-stand it, your guidance counselor suggested that because you're flunking everything at school. She also thinks you have some emotional problems that you're blocking out.

"You're in our hands now. The authorities are going to start making some choices for you. You decided that when you walked out of that clothing store with the stolen merchandise. Up until now you have chosen not to go to counseling. When you got yourself nailed, you automatically lost some of the opportunity to make choices. We'll see to it that the court sends you for help. You'll be working with a counselor twice a week and you'll be going to a group session. It's pretty cut and dry, Cory. We're about to force some help down your throat whether you like it or not. Your parents, or at least one of them, will come in once a week for some counseling, also. The counseling is going to take place for the family because problems occur as a family."

"I've tried to do my best." Margaret stroked her own arm and felt as if she were going to cry. "I honestly didn't know Cory was doing anything like this. I only knew she was miserable. I just didn't know how to reach her. Oh, Lord." Margaret put her hand to her forehead. "What a mess. What a terrible mess all of this is turning out to be."

"No one is blaming anyone, Mrs. Webber. I'm not saying that you caused any of these problems. We're not going to be looking so much at who caused what. What we're going to be looking at is how do we get everyone on track. Both of you have to quit burying your problems. Communication is the key as we all know. Unfortunately, almost no one does anything about it." Dave made some notes on a scrap of paper and put the paper inside Cory's file. "I won't be the one breathing down your neck, Cory. More than likely the juvenile officer working with you and your family will be Lola Montez. She's good people, as we say around here." Dave walked toward the door.

Margaret tapped Cory on the shoulder and indicated that she should get up and follow her. "Is this all there is to this? Are we free to go now?"

"Not quite. You're going to have to go through intake. Lola will be assigned to you at that time. They'll give you a schedule for the counseling. There are going to be some papers to sign. No, Mrs. Webber, you aren't free to go just yet. Keeping kids on the straight and narrow takes a lot more time than we'd all like to admit."

As many times as Margaret tried on the way home, she could not interest Cory in talking about what had happened or why she had taken the clothes. Cory would not talk about Matt, and she would not talk about the counseling that Lola Montez had explained to them both. Later that night Cory refused to talk to her father on the phone. Her only comment to Margaret was that if her father had cared anything about her, none of this would have happened in the first place.

Over the next several days Margaret held to one hope, and that hope was that the juvenile authorities would now be able to help her reach Cory. Margaret could see that this time things were different than all the other times in the past. Refusing to eat, staring blankly into space, closing herself off in her room, and flunking every subject at school were too many things to be happening in too short a period of time. Margaret had found it far easier to deal with the screaming and the pouting than she did with the empty stare that made Cory seem as if she were in a coma that allowed her only to move but not to speak, think, or feel.

Several times Margaret had read the literature that Lola Montez had given her. She wanted to understand what it was she and Cory would be doing over the next few months. Cory's father had called every night to see how Cory was. Each night Cory refused to talk with him. Margaret took it upon herself to tell Cory through her closed door that her father had called, that he supported the counseling program, and that he would be glad to attend the sessions or to do whatever he could to help. "He said he loves you, Cory. He'll be there for you, just as I'll be there, if you need us. Do you hear me, Cory? Just answer me. Just say yes or no." Margaret leaned her head closer to the door, hoping she would pick up some type of response. Any type of response. There was none.

After work Margaret hurried right home to be with Cory. She prepared the evening meal that Cory picked at. All through the meal Margaret made the effort to go right on talking about work and what was going on in the world as if Cory were listening and as if she would respond. She never said one word about the fact that Cory had quit her job and had already missed two days of school in one week.

Margaret did nothing to add to the pressures that she felt Cory was enduring. There was no way that Margaret could explain to her daughter that her own life was filled with pain because her child felt pain. The best that Margaret could do was to try to say a few words of support and to at least tell Cory that she cared.

"We've had our differences, Cory. All parents and their children have problems. Me and your father are going to try to work this out with you." She bent over the chair where Cory sat. "Someday when you have your own children you'll understand how much a mother loves her children. The pain that you're feeling, Cory, I feel, too." Margaret squeezed Cory's shoulders and moved away so that Cory wouldn't see her crying.

The day before Margaret and Cory were to attend the first group session for the parents and the offender, Margaret was summoned by her employer and told that someone wanted to talk to her. Margaret could feel her heart racing as she sped toward the office where her visitor awaited her. Her first thought was that Cory might have harmed herself. Margaret didn't know whether to feel relief or fear when she saw Dave Marlowski pacing inside the small office. Margaret put her fingers to her throat and took a deep breath before she put her hand on the doorknob. "Please don't tell me anything terrible. I don't think I can deal with any more bad news."

Dave felt sorry for her. He believed there were too many parents who didn't care whether their children were loose on the streets, locked up in detention, or classified as runaways. They simply were glad to be free of the responsibilities of taking care of youngsters whom they could not control. Margaret Webber obviously was a mother who cared. She just didn't know what to do and she was unable to reach her child.

"Cory was picked up again this afternoon. About one o'clock. She didn't make it to school today."

Margaret leaned against the wall before groping her way to a chair. "Picked up for what?"

"Same thing. Only this time we're talking about something more serious. Cory repeated exactly what she had done before. I mean she walked in the store and made no secret that she was stealing. When the manager tried to stop her outside the store, Cory kept swinging at him. It's not like the guy got hurt or anything, but the fact remains, Cory attacked him. I don't like to add this on, but Cory made matters worse by trying to pull away from the arresting juvenile officer. Cory is hell bent on doing something to get herself shipped off to juvenile detention. She couldn't have planned it better."

"Oh, my God. It's like this girl I knew has disappeared out of my life. I don't even know this child who robs stores and hits people. Cory is not that kind of youngster. Cory pouts and gets angry. Cory just doesn't do things like this. Mr. Marlowski, you work with kids all the time. Is this normal? Are teenagers going to act like this? Should I have expected my child to do things like this?"

"There aren't two fingerprints that are alike, and there aren't two teenagers that are alike. I can tell you this, Mrs. Webber, Cory is sending out a message because she's not trying to get away with anything. She's trying to get caught. Right now I don't know if the kid has got it in her head that she needs to be punished and by God she's going to get herself punished come hell or high water. She might be so angry that she wants to get back at someone, and the best way to get back is to get herself in trouble with the police. Sort of disgrace the family or some friend. Who knows what's going on in that girl's head. She probably doesn't even understand it herself."

"What's going to happen now?" Margaret let out a deep sigh. She was grateful that he seemed to care about what happened to Cory. It was as if Margaret had a partner or a friend who would help her even though there were no answers to the problem at hand.

"Her actions wiped out some more choices. Last time the court and the juvenile authorities would listen to me. I recommended family counseling and some individual counseling for Cory. I suggested the school counselor be kept informed so that she could monitor Cory's behavior at school. Everyone was perfectly happy to accept my recommendation because we already have wall-to-wall kids sitting it out in detention. Everyone is elated when we come across a candidate who might be helped *without* having to be locked up. There aren't going to be any ears that are going to listen to me this time. I might have been able to pull it off if we were just talking about shoplifting again. We're not. She attacked the manager and she kicked a police officer. We're moving into the big time, Mrs. Webber. What Cory has done is very serious. I can pretty well guarantee you that Cory is going to be sent to detention."

Margaret gulped again and again as she struggled to ask the questions for which she feared the answer. "When you say *detention*, you mean Cory is going to be sent away?"

"It's nearby. She'll get home visits." Dave put his hands on Margaret's shoulders. "One of the toughest things a parent has to deal with is knowing that his or her child is going to be locked up. It's not easy on the youngster, either. Until they hear the keys turning, they can't get it through their heads what it's like not to be able to turn around and walk out."

"Locked up! She's a child. You don't lock up children."

Dave saw no sense in telling Margaret that some children did things that were far worse than what many adults would ever think about doing. He believed that some children needed to be locked up. He was not sure that Cory was one of them, but the choice was no longer his. Her actions had carried her in that direction. Now she would be removed from her home, taken before the juvenile authorities, and locked up. "The laws don't always fit the crimes, Mrs. Webber. And the laws sometimes have a way of being blind to the weird circumstances. Nevertheless, if we start skirting around the laws because there is some strange situation, we'd sure have a mess on our hands."

Margaret only half listened. All she could see was Cory's forlorn face. Margaret's hands trembled thinking about what it would be like for her only child to be locked up behind bars with criminal-like children. "Is there nothing I can do? Get a lawyer. Maybe I can fight this thing. Delay what's going to happen until Cory can get herself together. There has to be something I can do to help my daughter."

He wished he could make her tears go away and he wished she was not going to have to face what he knew was ahead. "If it makes you feel any better, Mrs. Webber, many times the best thing parents can do for their kids is to make them see the consequences of their behavior. Cory is about to see that. As much as you don't want it to happen, Cory is just a short distance away from seeing what occurs when you make lousy choices."

CHAPTER FIVE

For the first time in several weeks Cory had feelings. Her muscles were tight and her head whirled as she felt fear deep inside every part of her body. Somehow when she sat before the judge and the juvenile officers and her mother held her hand, Cory knew she was still in a familiar place. When the gray van pulled up at the back of the downtown detention center things began to change. She stood in line with the six other juvenile offenders and waited for the woman in jeans and the blue flowered blouse to signal that they were to leave the building.

The driver came around and opened the van doors. The woman said her name was Nancy Lamb. Then she motioned for all the youngsters to get in the van and to fasten their seatbelts. It had been two hours since Cory had said goodbye to her mother. The two hours were much longer than any other two hours had ever been. Cory did not want to talk to the other six teenagers who waited in the large, empty room at the end of the juvenile court. Nor did she want to listen to their stories about all the terrible things that awaited them at Springdale Center. Some told how there were beatings if anyone talked back to teachers or counselors. One mentioned how she heard that this boy had secretly been sent from Springdale Center to an adult prison and his parents didn't even know where he was.

Until Cory had left juvenile court and had been taken to the waiting room, she had given very little thought to where she was going. Her mind was so deliberately empty, she could not even think how she had ended up in the large room with the tan walls and the delinquent youngsters.

The girl named Ginger turned around and asked Cory, "How come you're here? You don't look like a trouble-maker."

From the driver's seat in the van Nancy called out, "You were all told to be quiet in the van. This isn't some school outing. Cut the chit-chat." She looked as stern as it was possible to look. She didn't like some of the things that she had to say or do in her role as a counselor at Springdale, yet, she knew for the sake of what was ahead, they all had to learn to obey and to follow every rule whether they liked or didn't like the rule. "Turn around in your seats and take in the scenery. You're not going to be seeing any shops for quite a while to come."

Cory was frightened both by what Nancy said and the way she said it. Maybe what the others had said about the beatings and being sent to prison were true. Now Cory made a deliberate effort to think about her mother and their apartment. She wanted to think about anything except where she was going. Cory looked down at her wrist where her watch had been. All their jewelry, watches, and money had been taken away and put in canvas bags labeled with their names. When the tall boy had asked what right anyone had to take what was his, Nancy answered that he had lost his rights when he went through the juvenile system.

Without a watch, Cory could only estimate that they

had been traveling for about forty minutes or an hour. The swaying of the van made her sleepy. The instant her head dropped from nodding asleep, she woke up startled with the realization that she was on a van being transported to a detention center. The stores and shops had disappeared a few miles back and all Cory saw was open countryside. Like the others, Cory shifted around in her seat and tried to imagine what was ahead. In another half hour the van turned off the main highway and traveled for a little while on a blacktop road. Then the driver turned onto a gravel road. A few miles up the road they all saw the sign that said *Springdale Center.*

Perspiration broke out on Cory's hands as the bus drove beneath the sign and wound up the hill. Dust swirled up around the windows despite the early fall rains. The first thing Cory saw were teams of young people playing volleyball. There was some sense of relief that some of the horrible things that she had heard about Springdale could not be true if those who were confined to the center were playing volleyball.

Nancy spoke out as the bus pulled up in front of the administration building. "We've just passed the outdoor recreation area. You can see we do not chain our residents to trees as you've probably heard we do." She waited until the van came to a stop before unfastening her seatbelt and opening the door. "I will be taking you into the administration building and the Office of the Main Torturer, as Mrs. Francine Knight is often called. Mrs. Knight is going to have a long talk with all of you, and you had best pay attention. The more you do as you've been told to do, the happier we'll all be. Now come out the side door and move forward to that white door. Make a real point of keeping your mouths shut while you're doing what I asked." With that she hopped out of the van and waited for the four boys and three girls to get out of the van.

They were no sooner inside the door when Nancy said to a well-built and very athletic looking man, "They are all yours." Nancy turned to the group. "This is Martin. Martin chomps on juvenile offenders who don't stay in line. Isn't that right, Martin?"

He smiled at her and the youngsters. Martin motioned for them to follow him. "Down this way." They followed him down a long, clean corridor to a large room. "Mrs. Knight," he said to the woman who stood at the front of the room, "these are the new arrivals." His arm swung out to the left to indicate they were to take seats up close to Mrs. Knight.

None chose the front row. They all dropped back so that they were in front of Martin but as far from Mrs. Knight as they could get. Though the seats were spread out over several rows, the seven of them sat close together as if to get comfort from each other.

"I am Francine Knight. I will be Mrs. Knight to you even though you will commonly hear other staff members call me *Francine*. You will find your own nickname for me, none of which will be flattering to me. With that settled, may I say I welcome you despite the fact you don't want to be here. I don't want to be here myself. If there were no juvenile offenders, perhaps I could go out and get a job helping the elderly. Since young people go on committing crimes, there is a need for places such as Springdale and there's a need for people such as myself.

"Most of the talking is going to be done by me. Martin is going to pass out some pencils and a few pieces of paper. As I speak, if you think of questions you can write them down. When I'm all done speaking, if you still have questions that haven't been answered, I'll spend about fifteen minutes answering them. So let's begin. You might not know what a philosophy is; however, every church and business and school and detention center has a philosophy. A philosophy is the thing that you more or less believe in. People think, act, and behave according to their philosophy. Your philosophy, for whatever reason, was you could break the law and get away with it. The philosophy of Springdale is we are fed up with those who break the law. During the next six months, nine months or year, or depending how long you're going to be staying with us, you are going to see our philosophy come to life. We figure that's all the time we have to get you straightened out so that you don't come back to Springdale or move on to bigger and better things and get sent to the maximum security detention center for the really hard-to-get-along-with young people. Then, of course, we'd like to prevent your moving on to the *walls*, as the prison is called. And, no, we don't sneak in on you in the middle of the night and ship you off to prison as rumor has it."

Mrs. Knight poured herself some water. Cory realized that she was thirsty herself and would also like a drink. It bothered her that she didn't have the freedom to get a glass of water when she wanted one. Cory's eyes never left Mrs. Knight as she drank the water and then moved closer to where they all sat.

"After you leave this room you will go to intake. You're going to be given some clothes to wear. You won't have to worry about style and color. You'll all be wearing jeans and light blue denim shirts. That way we don't have to worry about anyone wanting anyone else's clothing. Sometimes difficult problems have very simple solutions. For two days you'll be placed in isolation except for meals. Isolation is not pleasant and we don't expect you to like it. You'll find we're not too much into what you might like or not like. While in isolation you should give some heavy-duty thought to how much time you might like to spend in isolation. That's where you're going if you can't learn to get along with your peers, your supervisors, teachers, and counselors.

"At the end of the two days you will be put in a dorm for a week. Boys in the dorm on the right. Girls on the left. During that seven day period you are to take a careful look at all the other young people here, and I can guarantee they'll be taking a careful look at you. You're going to be picked by a team. The teams know the only hope of getting out of here is to get the rules straight, obey them, shape up, help yourself while others are trying to help you, and don't get anyone else in trouble. The last thing they want on their team is a troublemaker. Each and every one of you can get the entire team in trouble. That means they *all* lose privileges. They all get punished because of what you do. You might not think that's fair, but like I said, we're not always overjoyed with what you think. The rule is you have to be on a team. Another rule is the team has to work together because that's what life is: Pulling along and helping each other. It also can mean dragging each other down. Whether you know it or not, you are known by the company you keep. If you hang out with rats, people think you're a rat. Not one of the teams wants a rat.

"You're going to have to look at the team members to try to figure out whether you think you can get along with them or not. They'll be doing the same thing. At the end of seven days they might pick you and you might not want to be on their team. If you can talk your way off their team and onto another team, more power to you. If you can't, you're stuck with them. You're in trouble if no one wants you. Until some team wants you, you're a Wanderer. Wanderers just wander in the Day Room. That means no television, no recreation. No nothing. The reason you're doing nothing is that for seven days you gave off some kind of vibes that scared others off. You look and smell like trouble and no one here wants trouble. You'll have another seven days to get it together and to hope the others see some good qualities in you that will make you acceptable to them. We've had a few who were Wanderers for as long as a month or two. That was their choice, and believe me, you don't get too many choices here.

"Once you get on a team, you can't be put off no matter what you do. That's why each team is pretty careful about who they select. They're stuck with you. They've already learned that at Springdale, once you make a decision, you have to live with the consequences whether they are good or bad. Decisions lead to problems, and you darn well better learn how to solve problems because problems are going to be a part of your life. In fact, *you* can be the problem.

"I'm not going to spend any time explaining the rules for getting along at Springdale. For a few days you're not going to be doing much thinking. You're going to be watching. You watch what the others do. If they sit, you sit. If they go outside, you go outside. If you look at someone and they appear to be doing something that doesn't look right to you, then you better have the good sense to look at someone else and copy what he or she is doing. We don't want you doing much thinking for about a week. Watch. Take my word for it. Just watch. Once you get on a team, you'll be doing more thinking than you've ever done in your life. You'll be thinking about everything you do because your actions can not only cause you trouble, they can get eight other people in trouble. There's nothing worse than when you have to deal with a half dozen teenagers who are ticked off at you.

"As to why you're here, everyone is going to find that out sooner or later. You can lie if you want, but eventually everyone will know the truth. In the meantime you can give anyone any answer you choose to give them. Believe me you're better off telling the truth because everyone loves rumors. For those of you who come from rotten homes, and many kids do, I can say I'm sorry that you got cut those kind of cards. But we at Springdale are offering you a chance. We can't undo the rotten home or the rotten parents, but we can offer you some help in how to cope with rottenness and how to save yourself from further trouble. Some of you came from nice homes and the only rotten one in them was you. We, and your family, aren't sure how you got that way because they tried and things didn't work out right. You still got in trouble. We know that you have gripes, complaints, raw deals, fair deals, parents who drink, and parents who have sold everything they own to help you. We'll help you shape up if you'll give us a try. If not, send us your address when you get locked up behind the walls and we'll send you a Christmas card."

As suddenly as she had started speaking, she stopped. Mrs. Knight moved back to a table and sat down. She waited a few minutes, taking in the dead silence. "Any questions?" She looked over the group for only a second. Without waiting for questions she said, "I thought not. Take them away, Martin. Let's get them settled in at their new home." Mrs. Knight disappeared through a door to the left.

Cory sat frozen in her chair. She only moved when Ginger poked her and motioned for her to get up. "My God! That's a horrible woman. I hope I never even see her again."

Martin tapped Ginger on the shoulder. "My advice is to follow her advice. Come on." His step was quick as he moved out the door and led them down the hall to the counter where they were to get their clothes.

The young girl behind the counter smiled. "I'm Tersea. Would you write your names down and give me your underwear sizes, and your clothes sizes? Then if you'd go over there and pick out shoes from those racks. You'll need some kind of sporty shoe and a pair of boots. Make sure they're really comfortable. Walk around in them. If you make the wrong choice, that means you either have sore feet or you walk around barefoot. If you're barefoot, you have to stay inside. The teams will be looking to see if you walk funny or anything like that because you were warned to think about your shoes." She smiled at Martin. "Am I covering it all, Martin?"

"Doing fine, Tersea. Just fine."

"So anyhow," Tersea continued, "don't just grab any pair. This is the first decision you're making. Better make a good one. You want to do everything you can to show the teams that your head is screwed on right." Tersea let out a deep sigh and smiled again. "I just got this job about four days ago and I want to get everything right."

Martin stood next to the shoe racks and watched them look for their sizes. He noted which of the seven tied the shoes all the way and walked around in both shoes. Gordon found his size, slipped his foot into a sneaker and then took a pair of boots that were the same size as the sneaker. Tersea said nothing about boots fitting differently than sneakers. Gordon, like the others, had been warned. Without giving it any additional thought, Martin knew that within two days Gordon would have sores on his feet from the boots that would slide up and down, rubbing the skin raw on his heel.

Tersea called their names and handed them a stack of clothing made up of three shirts, two pairs of jeans, seven pairs of socks and a change of underwear for every other day. "Someone might try to steal these. Everyone isn't as honest as they look," she said as she shrugged her shoulders.

Cory and the others again followed Martin down a corridor to a stairwell. A doctor waited to exam each of them and to check what information was available on their history of inoculations and general health. Then Martin moved them down another hall where the boys were separated from the girls. A woman named Angela greeted Cory, Ginger and the girl who said her name was Patrice. "You'll each be assigned an isolation room. I can tell you that you're not supposed to yell back and forth, but most of them do. When you do and someone catches you, you'll be asked to stop. I suggest you stop." Angela slid keys around on her ring and opened the doors that were painted a light pink. The soft color did nothing to take away from the fact that the doors were steel and that the only opening in the doors was a square foot window covered with bars.

"Cory Webber your room is 115. Ginger Montgomery, you'll be in 117, and Patrice Arquette, I have you down for the end room which is 119. You can change into your clothes now. You missed the regular lunch, but someone will be by to get you in about 30 minutes. Usually the first day you just get a sandwich and some soup. Don't judge all the meals by what you get today. The food isn't bad even though the kids complain endlessly that they are being fed poison. Fold up your street clothes and they'll be picked up and put with your other belongings."

Cory stepped into the small room. Once again she felt sick to her stomach when she heard the door shut and the key turn. She stood there facing the door. Her hand reached for the knob that she continually kept turning. Cory was unable to believe that she would be locked in this room for two days. The walls were painted the same light pink as the door. Up near the top of the room there was another barred window that was held open with a stick. Next to the small bed there was a nightstand and a small lamp. On the walls there were woven loops from which four hangers hung. Cory started to hang up the clothes that she had worn on the trip to Springdale. Then she remembered that she was to fold up her clothes and have them ready for Angela. A shiver ran down Cory's back as she thought she already was very frightened that she might do anything that would break a rule or that would make her unacceptable to a team.

After she had changed into the jeans and denim shirt, Cory tried to look into the little mirror that was on the nightstand. The shirt looked very drab, making Cory's face appear even more pale than it was. She reached into the paper bag that contained a few of the personal things that she had been allowed to keep. Cory took out her comb and brush and ran both through her straight brown hair. Then she dabbed a little blush on both cheeks. Checking her appearance once again in the mirror, Cory still felt that she looked sick.

Nothing more could be done to improve the way she looked. Suddenly Cory thought that it didn't matter how she looked in this terrible place. She thought about the other girls whom she had seen as she moved down the halls and from place to place at the center. Some of the girls had on makeup and fancy clips or headbands. Other girls looked as plain and drab as Cory. Perhaps they, like Cory didn't care how they looked.

The bed was much harder than the bed that Cory was used to. Cory bounced slightly to see if she thought she could sleep on the bed. As Cory lay down she was sure that she had heard Ginger call out. The choice was not to answer her. Cory put her hands beneath her head and fell back on the pillow. Her eyes wandered from blank wall to blank wall. She seemed unaware that tears fell as she lay there staring up at the ceiling. It was easy to understand why they called this area *isolation*. Cory felt totally alone. Totally deserted.

CHAPTER SIX

Cory wasn't sure whether it pleased or upset her that Ginger chose to attach herself to Cory. During the first week the new arrivals were allowed to sit wherever they wanted to sit as long as their presence was acceptable to the others at the table. It was unusual for those at the table to turn anyone down because they wanted whatever opportunities they had to get to know those who had just arrived. Cory followed the instructions she had been given and asked permission before sitting down. Ginger said, "I guess I'll just sit with you guys." Cory shot a look at the others to see if they approved or disapproved of Ginger's boldness and her obvious violation of asking first if it were all right before sitting down.

The conversation at the table didn't include Cory or Ginger until Jose introduced himself. His skin was dark and he had a long scar on the right side of his face. Cory felt uncomfortable when he told them his name and continued to stare at them. If Cory had seen him on the street, she would have been frightened of him.

"I'm the coordinator for Team 8," Jose said as he sprinkled a large amount of pepper on his macaroni. "We don't have names. Huh, guys." His dark eyes moved from one to the other. "We're all some kind of number here. Mrs. Knight says getting used to being nothing more than a number is good for us in case we decide to go on being offenders." He smiled and didn't look nearly as mean. Then he mocked how Mrs. Knight spoke. "If you go on being an offender, you'll be nothing more than a number for the rest of your life. Besides," his voice changed tone, "letting our teams have names makes us too much like a gang. Man, that woman don't know nothing about gangs. Now me, I know all about gangs."

The boy at the end of the table leaned forward. "Doesn't, Jose. That woman *doesn't* know anything about gangs. You gotta keep working on getting that English correct or we're all going to flunk English usage."

"Hey, look who's talking." Marvella pointed her fork at Jeff. "You and your *gottas*. It's *have to*. I'm the only one who speaks correctly."

"So, Miss Rich Bucks, you came from one of them families that drinks tea out of cups and who sends their kids to tutors. No such luck in my family. We stole to eat."

"Come off it, Jeff," Marvella shook her head. "Mrs. Knight said it doesn't matter what our family backgrounds are. She said we have a chance now whether we were rich or poor. I really get tired, I mean really tired of listening to how poor your family is. It's a bore. Pass the milk, please."

"You, whatever your name is, pass the milk." Jose nodded toward Cory.

Cory quickly grabbed the pitcher and lifted it so quickly that milk sloshed over the lip of the pitcher. "I'm sorry." Cory felt her face turning red.

Ginger nudged her. "You don't have to apologize, Cory. You didn't mean nothing by it. It was an accident.

Right?" Ginger looked at the others.

"So who said anything?" Jeff put his arms on the table and stared Ginger down. Then he said, "Now what do you guys have to offer? I'm a nobody on Team 5, but I'd like to know about the both of you. I figure Ginger here for a mouth that never stops. What's your story, Milk Slopper?"

Marvella frowned. "You just told her no one is judging her and then you file a case on her. You're stupid."

"Is that name calling?" Jeff turned on Marvella. "No name calling. That leads to arguments. That's...that's... What does Angela say name calling is?"

Jose answered, " When you make a person feel worse about himself or herself it's demeaning. Man, that lady would go nuts out on them streets. I got a name for everyone and none of them are good." Jose broke out laughing. "The Terrible Torturer would drop her teeth if she heard what we call each other."

"And what's the point," Marvella commented. "Like the Terrible Torturer says, if we carry our old ways out of here, nothing is going to change when we get back home. So quit calling each other names."

Jeff shook his head in disgust. "Marvella here has been totally and completely brainwashed. She actually believes every bit of the baloney they stuff down our throats."

Marvella stopped eating and waited a minute. Then turned to Ginger and Cory. "It can go either way. It just so happens I don't want to end up back here. I honest to God want to get myself turned around. I'm tired of all the messes I'm in. I was a runaway. Four times I ran away and every time I got myself in a bigger mess than the last time. It's scary out on those streets. Creeps and weirdos are every place. That's not what I want to do. Sure I try to listen to these people. I really believe this is my last chance. I'm seventeen and I better do something. What they're telling me here sounds about as good as anything I've heard so far."

They all sat in silence for several minutes. Then Jeff once again asked Cory about herself. Cory merely answered *yes* when he wanted to know if it were true that she was at Springdale for stealing and kicking a police officer.

Ginger's eyes opened in surprise. "You kicked a *police officer*! Holy cow! I sure never would have figured you for doing something like that. Now me, I'm more the type to whack one of those know-it-alls."

Jose eyed Ginger, taking note that by her own admission she would attack an authority figure. Whereas Ginger's boldness made Jose nervous, it was Cory's silence and her withdrawn ways that bothered him. There were only a few minutes left before the noon bell would ring and they'd return to class, yet, he thought he would do as the counselors had suggested they all do: When one of the residents was doing something that was harmful to themselves, the wisest thing was to tell them in a kind, rational way what he or she was doing. Jose thought of Martin's advice, "When someone doesn't know that what he or she is doing wrong, it's pretty hard for them to stop doing it."

"I'm going to say something to you guys and you can take it for what it's worth. You, Red," he addressed Ginger by a name that he associated with her bright red hair, "I'd worry about having you on my team because you didn't ask permission to sit down. That means you don't follow rules and I don't want anyone on my team who breaks the rules. I got this gut feeling that you think you can say anything you want to say. You gotta think around here before you run your mouth. I don't think you're going to think. I'd be willing to bet you'll say something that will get us all in trouble.

"And you...what's your name again?"

"Cory."

"You're like some little, dinky scared mouse. Look at you. All hunched over. I don't think those things are so good. You're not going to talk up in group. I got you figured for sitting there and saying nothing. Just walking around scared to do anything. What do you guys think? Would you want her on your team?"

Before any of them could answer Ginger spoke up. "Where do you get off telling me and Cory what all is wrong with us? If you're so perfect, maybe you can explain to me why you're at the biggest detention center in this state. You know they don't bring you out here for talking too loud. And those scars on your face, Jose, you got them out on the streets fighting. I've only been here a few days and I'm getting fed up listening to all this garbage about doing this for a team and that for a team. The teams can go to hell. I don't care if I ever get on a team. I didn't need anyone before and I sure don't need anyone now. Isn't that right, Cory?"

Cory knew nothing of Ginger's needs. She only knew that it made her nervous when Ginger tried to include her in any plans that would get them rejected by a team. "I don't know, Ginger. We have to be on a team."

Marvella scooted her chair closer to Cory's, ignoring Ginger. "You understand we have to be careful who we end up with. You learn here that almost nothing can be done alone. Whether you're carrying a rock or building a bridge, you have to work with others. Our counselor told us how it's going to be when we get jobs. All day long we're going to have to work with people and if we can't get along, we could lose our jobs. I don't think Jose is being all that hard on you, Cory. He's just trying to tell you that sometimes the ones who keep to themselves are even harder to get along with than girls like Ginger. You know what I'm trying to say?"

"I guess."

"That's just what Jose means. You answer me 'I guess.' What do you really think or what do you really feel?"

Ginger hit the table with her knife. "For crying out loud. You're going to get Cory bawling or something. She just got here and she's scared. We don't know anything about her. For all we know she's got a father who beats her like mine does. What you guys are saying is enough to put anyone over the edge. For all we know maybe she's been beaten so many times that she's afraid to talk."

Though the reason for her not speaking out was not correct, Cory felt some sense of closeness with Ginger for the way she defended her. "My father didn't ever beat me. He just abandoned me and my mother."

"See." Ginger stared at Jose in a challenging way. "Her dad dumped her and her mother. Stuff like that will shut a kid up."

Jeff interrupted, "We're getting off the track. No one asked about what our parents did or didn't do. All Jose wants to know is if Cory is going to be dead weight who never comes up with any solutions or ideas for the team."

Before anyone could say anything else the noon bell rang. Each of them stood up and took their dishes to the kitchen area and their trays to the stacks. As Cory left the dining hall she did as she had done on the first day. She followed a group of other students to classes. For the first week it didn't matter to which classes the new arrivals went. Cory was too worn out to leave the first class after lunch so she just sat in the same room until the next class arrived. One of the students asked, "Aren't you in here from the last class?"

Cory only nodded. "Is that going to go against me? I mean in getting on a team."

The student responded, "It seems kind of nutty just to sit in here." Then he raised his hands in the air. "Don't ask me. I just got on a team last week myself. These teams run me nuts. I'm Sean. We're supposed to introduce ourselves and shake hands. My counselor, Martin, calls those kinds of things *social amenities*. Darn. I can't believe I said that. Social amenities." He grinned and sat down in the seat behind Cory. "I'm on Team 5."

"I met a Jeff who's on Team 5."

"Yeah. Jeff Carberry. He's okay. The team coordinator is Marsha. What a bi..." Sean stopped himself, remembering that he was not to use profanity. "I'm telling you she's hard to get along with. She must have every rule from all over the world memorized. Cindy told me that when we vote again on our coordinator that Marsha can kiss the job goodbye. From what the other guys on the team say, Marsha started out okay and now she's gone nuts with power. We got the right to get rid of our leaders if they're not what we want. Martin says that's the way our government works, and that's the way it works at Springdale. What are you here for?"

Cory still felt uncomfortable admitting what she had done. "Committing a crime like everyone else."

"I broke into a school and stole two computers. That's two separate times I did that. Heck, I don't even know how to work a computer." Sean turned around in his seat as he realized the classroom had filled up. Out of the side of his mouth he whispered, "I'll talk to you later. I might put in a good word for you to get on Team 5."

A small feeling of excitement traveled through Cory. What Sean said was the first positive thing she had heard about herself since she arrived at Springdale. A week later when Team 5 picked her, Cory was never sure whether it was Jeff or Sean who had spoken up for her. That she didn't become a Wanderer as Ginger became was a relief to Cory. She didn't understand why, but she felt sorry for Ginger. She also felt a sense of disloyalty to the girl who had befriended her. Cory understood that Ginger must feel abandoned just as Cory had felt abandoned when Nicole and Matt had deserted her. At the risk of getting a demerit for Team 5, Cory stopped by the dayroom where Ginger spent her idle time as a Wanderer.

"I'm sorry you didn't get picked, Ginger. I really am. Can I get you a magazine or something? Maybe a candy bar?"

"We can't eat candy and we can only read school books." As much as Ginger prided herself on standing up for her right to say what she wanted to say, she envied Cory's having been picked for a team. Ginger looked around at the other Wanderers who sat sleeping in chairs in the dayroom. "You can see how lively my company is." Ginger leaned forward in the chair. "These are the creepiest, most horrible people you can imagine. Look at that one over there." Ginger nodded toward a rail thin boy. "I think that one is nuts. He thumps his thumbs all day long. Then it's like he passes out. He scares me. If I get killed in here, you tell them that Skin and Bones did it. Now you better get out of here before someone catches you."

Cory knew that Ginger was right. "Ginger, will you

try? Do everything that you're supposed to do. Believe me being on a team isn't all that bad. This guy Sean is real nice to me. Cindy is great. I don't know the others too well except that Marsha, but everyone hates her. It will be okay, Ginger. You'll see. Just do whatever you're supposed to do and I'll bet you anything that next week you'll get on a team. Maybe you can even get on Team 5. I told Sean about you and he said he'd vote for you. I can't vote yet. I have to be here forty-five days before I can vote, but I'd sure vote for you if I could. Hang tough, girl. Okay."

Ginger felt touched that Cory ran a risk to speak to her. "Yeah. I'm going to give it a shot. Thanks."

Cory looked around and dashed out of the room. She didn't notice Martin who had both seen and heard the girls talking. He made no effort to write down the violation. He believed the advice that Cory had given Ginger was good advice.

Cory entered the large enclosed porch where Team 5 met for their group sessions. Even though it had been over four weeks since Cory had arrived at Springdale, she still felt comfortable only if she sat between Sean and Cindy. What she knew of the others on Team 5 came from the group sessions because Cory spent very little time with them. She went on eating her meals with Marvella, Jose and Jeff, and she looked upon Sean and Cindy as the only others who seemed to know that she existed. When it came Cory's time to speak today, she was determined to say something in Ginger's favor.

Marsha opened the group session by handing out the week's assignments. Those who had kitchen detail groaned. There was not a resident who didn't complain about having to do kitchen detail because it involved so much scrubbing and very careful inspections to see that the job was done correctly. The emphasis on having a clean kitchen never stopped. Cory found that the requirements her mother had were far more lenient than those of the inspectors who moved through the kitchen looking for the smallest spattering of grease or for anything that didn't gleam.

Once Marsha had handed out the assignment that contained the names of each group member and what they were to clean over the weekend, she turned to Cory. "You've been here four weeks. It's time for you to begin paying back your debt to society."

Everyone in the group groaned. "Come on, Marsha, just get on with it." Jeff sighed and slumped in his chair. "You don't have to echo Mrs. Knight. No one wants to hear about their *debt to society*. We all got the drift. Let's just get on with it and help Cory figure out what she wants to do."

Cory knew about the *debt to society*. Everyone who came to Springdale had to pay back what they had dishonestly taken or had to make up for what they might have done to another person. The list of what they could do was fairly long and the money they earned for their work was less than what they could earn at any ordinary job away from Springdale. The residents had to go over their offense with a counselor and with their team. Together they totaled what the offense cost society. Each resident then had to contribute his or her earnings to pay off the debts. When possible, the money was given directly to the victim who had suffered the loss. When that was not possible, the money was turned over to the city's Victims of Crime program.

"Would any of you like to tell Cory what you do? Maybe that will give her an idea about some of the ways she can earn money. Let's see, Cory," Marsha glanced down at Cory's offense sheet, "you have it fairly easy. Everything you got caught stealing was returned. Then you estimated that you had stolen about five hundred dollars worth of things and you never got caught. Compared to some of us, paying back five hundred dollars is going to be easy."

"Wait a minute, Miss Mouth...Excuse me, Martin. I didn't mean to call her names. I honest to God didn't mean it." Jeff put his hands up in the air. "Wait a minute, Marsha. We're not supposed to judge each other about whether or not something is easy. Sure I have to pay back almost two thousand dollars, and compared to me, it might look easy for Cory, but who's to say what's easy or hard for someone else. You're violating one of our rights here and that's not to be judged by someone else."

"Get off it," Sean protested. "We're judging each other all the time. We start judging when we decide who's getting picked for a team. I'm not defending Marsha because I don't like what she said, either, but I sure don't want to hear how we're not supposed to judge each other. Near as I can tell we get up judging and we go to bed judging. It doesn't even make sense. Isn't that right, Martin?"

They all looked to their counselor. "We can get to that issue later. The issue at hand is getting Cory an assignment. If we leave that behind and get off on a discussion about judging people, we might not have any time left to get Cory going so she can earn what she owes."

Cindy tapped Cory on the shoulder. "You were a dope to admit the stealing. I mean the ones where you didn't get caught. We sure wouldn't have known. I think that was a stupid thing to do."

"Stupid or not," Sean defended Cory, "she was honest. You got to give her something for being honest. If anything, it shows we can trust her. Now let's get on with it."

Martin pulled over a chair and sat down amid the group. "Run it past her, Jeff, what you do."

"I work at this here place where old people go. Most of them are about ready to die and they don't got any families or nothing to help them. You see, I knocked this one old guy down when I took his wallet. That old man broke his hip. At this old folks place I work with people who got something wrong with their legs. Like they can't walk or nothing. I push them around in wheelchairs to the game room and..."

106

"Game room!" Gene laughed. "You mean to tell me those ancients play games? What kind of games can death warmed over play?"

"Cut it out, jerk." Jeff became defensive. "Those people like to play cards and get some exercise. You don't know nothing about those old people. They're pretty nice. They can't help it what happened to them. I got to admit, Cory, I like what I do. I go three times a week and I only have to go twice. I'm even going to this picnic with them on Saturday." Jeff glared at Gene. "For someone stupid, you sure think you know a lot. And," Jeff quickly added, "I didn't call him stupid. I just said he *was* stupid. There's a difference."

"Thank you, Jeff, for your description." Martin pointed to Gene. "You want to explain to Cory what you do, Gene?"

"Oh, now," Gene yawned, "it's as exciting as all get out. Every Saturday I get in the van and ride back to the city and work for Gadson Electronics. From eight to five. Whoopee!" Gene's facial expression never changed. "I stock inventory. I dust glass shelves. I wash windows. I vacuum floors. I sweep the sidewalk. You'd just love it, Cory. It's so exciting I can't stand it."

Martin turned toward Gene. "No one promised you an exciting job, Gene. We only said that you'd earn three bucks an hour. You made the choice and that's what you'll do until you pay back what you owe. Next time you might want to think it through a little before you make a choice to do something illegal."

Gene dropped his feet onto the floor and acted as if he were going to stand up. "Listen, I was told I'd be working around electronic equipment. That sounded okay to me. I didn't know I was going to be some kind of servant or slave."

Martin waved his hand toward the group. "I know this is a little off what we're talking about, but would any of you like to comment?"

The boy they called Winnie raised his hand. "First, Gene complains about everything so I don't think any of us should take him too seriously. I personally think he's headed for more trouble when he gets out of here. He follows the rules, but he doesn't believe in them, and..."

Martin put up his hand. "You're getting off track. I'd like some comment about Gene saying that he's some kind of servant or slave."

"Sure." Winnie rocked in his chair as he kept talking. "You got to understand that all inmates are more or less slaves. They work for almost nothing. We're *residents* rather than inmates, but we have to keep in mind if we end up in prison, we're going to work for nearly nothing for a long time to come. Gene, you broke into a store and smashed up a whole bunch of stuff. You owe for the things that you ruined. It's going to take you a long time to pay for everything you broke. You should have thought of that when you were breaking up the junk. You're not a slave. You owe, guy. You owe."

Martin nodded in agreement. "Winnie's right. You broke the law, Gene. You destroyed property that didn't belong to you. It never occurred to you how the owner was going to replace what you destroyed. To be whining and complaining about working off the debt tells me that in your head you still don't think you owe. Whether you like it or not, you owe, and that's why you mop floors and dust off glass shelves."

"I don't owe as much as you say. I'm going to be some old man or something before I ever get it paid off." Gene looked disgusted. He didn't like it at all that Martin and Winnie had turned on him. "Besides, we're not talking about me. We're supposed to be helping Mealy Mouth to figure out how *she's* going to pay her debt to society."

Martin glared at Gene for the name calling that he hated. "You're right," Martin agreed. "But that doesn't keep us from saying that we think you're a pain in the butt, Gene. Until you admit that you owe every dime that you're making, even if you're not making all that much, you're telling me that you have a long way to go before you start changing your ways. Now anyone else want to tell what they are doing?"

Cory raised her hand. "I think I know what I want to do. I saw this thing on the list that said you could work with kids. Like teaching them to read. I think I'd like to do that."

"And why do you think that?" Marsha asked.

"Because I don't have any brothers or sisters of my own

and I think it would be fun working with little kids." Cory
ignored the fact that she had a young stepbrother. No one
said anything because no one yet knew about the child that
Cory disliked so much.

"Hold on a minute, Cory," Martin turned to Cory. He
didn't mention to the group that Cory lied about not having
a brother. He'd call her on that one later on. For now he
carried the conversation in the direction he wanted it to go.
"First, you'll only be working with the younger children
two nights a week. That's not going to make them your
brothers or sisters. Your job won't be to find a sibling.
Your job will be to help with reading. Secondly, don't
approach these jobs as something that's fun. You heard
what Gene had to say. He sure doesn't think of his job as
fun, and you might find out that getting a ten-year-old kid
to read is not fun. You should approach the job mainly as a
means of earning money to pay back what you owe. You
start looking beyond that, and you're going to be disappointed."

"Whatever," Cory said as she shrugged her shoulders.
"It's what I want to do, anyhow." She lowered her head
before their stares made her change her mind.

"If you've thought about it, and if you're ready to stand
by your decision, so be it." Martin wrote down Cory's
assignment. "You'll enter the training program at
McKinley Elementary School next Wednesday. Like it or
not, you will have to stick with that program until you leave
here."

Cory leaned forward and raised her hand once more. "Could I say something?"

"That's why we have group," Martin smiled. "Give it all up so we know what's going on in your head."

"It's about Ginger."

"What about her?"

"No team has picked her yet, and I want to say something in her favor."

Winnie frowned. "Not anything in favor of getting her on this team. We got enough problems with Gene. We don't need another problem."

"Just shut up, Winnie." Cory surprised herself when she spoke so boldly.

Martin bowed his head so that they wouldn't see his smile. He didn't like Cory's choice of words, but he was glad to see that she was no longer as withdrawn and depressed. In the last week she had begun to show some of the anger that she felt. Away from the group Cory still remained timid and kept to herself. Within the group, though, she was beginning to speak up and to express herself. Those were signs that Martin looked for because they showed improvement in Cory's attitude. Martin scribbled some notes about Cory and then said, "At one time or another most of you have spoken up for someone else. Cory has that right now. We only have seven on the team. We have room for one more. What do you want to say in Ginger's behalf?"

"She's not nearly as bad as you guys think. I've had

lots of time to talk to Ginger. She's been beaten something terrible by her father. I mean she's got marks all over her back. I'd run away, too, if my dad did that to me. Even when she was a little kid she tried to yell at her dad and to stand up for herself. That's why she talks out so much. Ginger has been doing that for so long that she can't quit now. She needs our help. I think we're pretty selfish if we don't do something to help her."

Marsha looked surprised that Martin had let Cory say what she said. "Martin, I didn't think we were supposed to tell anyone else's personal story. What we know about ourselves is supposed to be our choice as to whether we tell or not. Cory's saying personal things about Ginger. That's not allowed."

Jeff waved his hand at Marsha. "Get off it. Cory's only trying to help."

"You can't help others until they help themselves," Marsha answered defiantly.

"Hold it." Martin silenced them. "Marsha is right. It's up to each one of you to tell your own stories, but we can't fault Cory for showing compassion for her friend. Without compassion for others, we can turn into some pretty cruel people. Let's just say that being a Wanderer is very difficult. It means being alone and isolated. No one wants that. Maybe I can suggest, Cory, that you show Ginger that you'll be her friend no matter what. Maybe that's what she needs now. The rest of us will try to be a little less harsh on her. Maybe the group will overlook some things and be willing to take a chance on Ginger." Martin looked from one to the other. "There's not a one of you who isn't a risk. You're risks because you broke the law. If you did it once, you can do it again. With that, we'll drop our discussion about Ginger."

Martin turned again to Cory. "Maybe this is your day. You were able to make a decision about how you were going to pay back your debt to society. Do you think you're ready to share your personal story yet?"

Cory lowered her head. She did not want to talk about any of her problems. "I don't think so."

"We can't start working out your problems until we know what they are, or at least what you *think* they are." Martin tried to coax Cory into speaking.

"So what's the big secret?" Gene glared at Cory. "Your story can't be any worse than ours."

Cory didn't want to tell them that the reason she didn't tell her personal story was that compared to what had happened to the others, her home life was not a bad one. When Cindy was twelve her mother began abandoning her for months at a time. Cindy had to find ways to feed herself and to beg people to take her in. Gene's father was an alcoholic who had turned Gene into a an alcoholic. Ever since Jeff was eight years old he had been sexually abused by his own uncle. Marsha had a similar home situation only it was her stepfather who had sexually abused her and her sister. The abuse was ignored and denied by Marsha's own mother. Sean's parents only worked from time to time. His family had been evicted nine times in one month, and when they finally began living in shelters, Sean was abandoned because there were no shelters that would take teenage boys.

Each week Cory listened to the others on her team. She'd see them pound their fists in rage or sit with tears rolling down their faces as they tried to tell of the horrible things that led to their finally being sent to Springdale. Cory thought about her own parents. The worst that could be said of either was that they didn't earn a great deal of money and Cory was denied some of the things that other young people had. Cory didn't always understand the mixed feelings she had toward her mother and father. Mainly, though, Cory had come to realize that she feared her mother might leave her just as her father had done, and since the birth of Rory, Cory was sure that the child would take all her father's love and that he wouldn't have any to give her.

"Well, Cory, you're going to have to bite the bullet sooner or later." Martin wasn't so much warning as reminding her. "It's all part of the program here. You have to spill it out."

"I said I don't think I can."

"Why?" Martin asked.

Cory twisted in her chair, wanting them to stop looking at her. "I'm ashamed. I don't want you to listen to me because I'm ashamed."

Jeff gently nudged Cory's foot with his own. "Listen,

we've all done some rotten stuff. You can't have done anything worse than me beating up an old man. That's something to really be ashamed of. You should hear some of the stories that get told here. No matter what you've done, we'll listen. Isn't that right, Martin?"

"That's right."

"Suppose, though, what happened to me isn't so bad. I mean I have two parents, but they're divorced. Neither one of them have ever hit me or abused me." Cory started crying. "I don't know what my problem is. When I listen to you guys, I don't think I've got anything to complain about. I'm just one of those whiners and complainers that you're always talking about."

Martin reached over and patted Cory on the knee. "Then let's hear what it is that you have to whine and complain about. You can't compare yourself to others. Each one of us has different needs and different problems. The point is, you ended up stealing. We have to get to the bottom of that or you could end up doing it again."

Cory shook her head. "I'm just not ready to talk about me."

Sean bent his head down so that he wouldn't have to look at Cory. He knew enough about his feelings to realize that he liked her. He liked her more than any girl he had ever met. He wanted her to be able to tell her story so that she would get better and so that she would be able to go home. After Martin called an end to the session, Sean walked down the hall with Cory. "I'm sorry you had such a rough time of it." He hoped that she would know he was sincere.

"I'm just such a mess, Sean." Cory brushed her brown hair back and bit her lip. "I always feel like I'm on the verge of crying. I wish I could be tough like some of these guys around here. They've been through so much, and you know what my biggest complaint is? You honestly want to know the only thing I have to complain about is my parents are divorced."

"Probably not, Cory. Millions of kids have parents who are divorced and they don't end up here. You've put some bad feelings some place inside you. You just don't know what the feelings are and where you put them." Sean reached down and touched Cory's hand. "I know we're not supposed to touch each other, but I just felt like I wanted to feel your hand."

Cory curled up her fingers so that they no longer touched Sean's. "Please don't do that." She felt uncomfortable at his closeness. "Don't ever touch me again. I don't want anyone touching me. Ever."

"That's what I mean, Cory. You got some queer feelings. I don't think you trust anyone. Sooner or later you have to trust people. I know I don't trust my mom and dad. They'll dump on me every chance they get, but I think I can learn to trust other people. I could learn to trust you."

"Stop it!" Cory turned on Sean. "Don't even say such things to me. You don't know anything about me."

"I know I really like you."

116

"Yeah. I've heard that before. My mom tells me she loves me. My dad is always saying how much I mean to him, but he spends all his time with that horrible Rory. And Matt, he..." Cory burst out crying. "I trusted someone once and he deserted me. He said he loved me and he didn't even help me. Don't talk to me about trusting people. I hate people." Cory backed away from Sean. Then she ran down the hall toward the dorm.

CHAPTER SEVEN

Margaret was waiting when Cory stepped off the van. For the first time in eight weeks Cory was home for a visit. Seeing her daughter made Margaret feel uneasy. The thing she most dreaded was that she would say the wrong thing and somehow upset Cory. Even the plans that she had made for the weekend with her daughter seemed wrong now. Margaret wanted them to go home together and then to go shopping and out to eat lunch at the mall. Thinking about the mall made Margaret nervous. She wasn't sure how Cory would behave in the mall. Being there might remind her of all the terrible things that had happened.

As Cory moved away from the van, Margaret smiled and waved. Then she threw her arms around her daughter and kissed her cheek. "Welcome home, sweetheart." Tears fell down Margaret's face. "I'm just so glad to see you."

The hostility that Cory felt simply would not go away. "Are you really glad I'm home? You mean my mom is happy to see her juvenile delinquent. I'd think you'd want to put a bag over my head so no one would see you kissing your little jail bird."

Margaret's hands shook. The weekend was not likely to go as she hoped. It would be a weekend of anger and that is not what Margaret wanted. "Your father is going to come by tomorrow. He found work. That's good, isn't it?" Margaret didn't wait for her daughter to answer. "He wants to take you and Rory to the amusement park. He thought you'd like that. It's supposed to be a nice day."

Margaret felt awkward searching for words that would keep the conversation going. Instead, Margaret walked up to Martin and signed the papers that he held out to her. Margaret scratched her signature across the release that said she would be responsible for seeing that Cory stayed within her custody and that she would be returned to the van by six o'clock tomorrow night for the trip back to Springdale. As Margaret leaned down to sign the paper she whispered to Martin. "Is she doing all right? I mean is she making some progress?"

Martin spoke up so that Cory could hear his answer as easily as Margaret. "Cory has a chip on her shoulder. It weighs her down. One of these days she's going to learn to dump some of that anger. Then she'll probably be okay. Until then, she'll walk stooped over because chips on shoulders weigh you down. Enjoy yourself, Cory." Martin moved closer to her. "Think about this weekend and what you do. We'll want to hear about it in group next Tuesday."

Margaret and Cory moved toward the curb where they waited for the bus. All the people and all the stores seemed overwhelming to Cory. It had been so long since she had seen so much activity. They took a seat at the back of the bus. Cory stared out the window at the young people walking in pairs or in groups down the street. The same feeling of envy that she always had came back to nag at her. She twisted her hands angrily as she fought the feeling that no matter where she was, she just didn't seem to belong.

The apartment seemed smaller and even more drab than Cory remembered it being. From the window Cory only saw other buildings crowded together. For a minute she thought about the trees and open spaces at Springdale. It surprised her that she recalled the country and the trees with fondness. "Do I have to be with you every second I'm home?" Cory flopped down on the couch and turned on the television.

"I don't suppose it has to be that way." Margaret didn't really understand what her daughter meant. "Is there something that you'd like to do? Something special?"

"Mainly I want to be left alone." Cory didn't understand how she felt because for several days she had looked forward to coming home and seeing her mother. Now that she was home, she felt resentment rising up in her about the little apartment and the fact that it contained nothing pretty or new. Though her mother didn't say anything to her, Cory could almost hear her talking about how to clean the kitchen properly or how she shouldn't be spending so much time in her room. "I know you're trying to help, Mom, but I think this first time you'd just be better off leaving me alone."

"I just hate to see you sit around all day. It might be better for you if you kept yourself occupied."

"One thing we're taught at Springdale, Mom, is how to use our time in a worthwhile way. Trust me to do that." Cory looked straight ahead at the television. Margaret had no way of knowing that Cory had already made plans for the day. She was simply waiting for the opportunity to slip away from Margaret and to get to the mall. Matt and Nicole would be at the mall because they always were at the mall by noon on Saturday. The only comfort Cory felt came from knowing that today she would get revenge for what they had done to her.

At eleven o'clock Cory picked up her purse and quietly slipped out of the apartment. She didn't give a thought to Margaret worrying about where she had gone or why. The bus came along at exactly ten minutes after eleven. By eleven-thirty Cory was in the mall and heading for the escalator where Matt and the others met each Saturday. She ignored the stares of students from school who by now knew that Cory had been sent away to a detention center. None of them even bothered to wave or to say a word to her. Their lack of attention didn't bother Cory this morning. She had more important things on her mind.

Up ahead she saw Matt. She had forgotten how nice looking he was, but his handsome face didn't change how she felt. His grin only made her feel rage. Nicole hung onto his arm, laughing and talking about nothing as she always did. With an angry boldness, Cory walked up to them both. "I see it's Saturday morning as usual." Cory attempted to smile.

"Cory!" Matt smiled and reached out for her. "Darn if it isn't Cory. How about this, Nicole? Cory's here. Did you get out or something? I thought you'd be gone for months. Didn't we, Nicole?"

"Don't ask me. I don't know anything about those places." Nicole acted no differently than she always acted. Innocent and disinterested.

"You two going shopping?" Cory did all she could to make herself seem interested in what they were going to do that afternoon. More than anything Cory wanted to entice them into shoplifting as they had done so many times on their Saturdays in the mall. "We don't get much at Springdale. I thought it might be nice to take a few things back with me. You understand, don't you? I figure you guys owe me that." Cory felt nothing but hatred for the both of them.

Nicole shot a glance at Cory. "Gosh, I'd think that as much trouble as you were already in that you wouldn't want to take any more chances. You must like living on the fringe."

"Sure. Why not?" Cory's stomach was in tight knots as she fought to control screaming at them both for the way they had betrayed her. "Well, are we going to plan something or not?"

"Why not?" Matt grinned. "I could use a little excitement this morning. You two want to work as a team, or you want me to work with one of you?"

"What are we going to get?" Cory walked along beside Matt. She looked at him and wondered how she ever could have loved him when now she couldn't stand the sight of him.

"Shoes. Let's get some good running shoes. I like those kind that you can pump air into and they fit perfect. I picked up a pair like that about a month ago. I had them until the shoelace broke." He burst out laughing. "There's no sense keeping shoes if a lace is broken." Matt turned down the left wing of the mall and moved toward the store where they sold expensive footwear. "We'll get some shoes for me. Then we'll see what you want, Cory. Believe me, we'll see that you go back with what you need." He reached over and took Cory's hand. "I'm really glad you're home. You might not believe me, but I'm sure happy that you're not upset with us anymore. I didn't like it when you were so mad at us. Nicole didn't, either."

Cory made an effort to smile back at him. She was sure that the way she gritted her teeth would give away her plans. "There's no sense holding a grudge." She backed away from Matt and carefully eyed the location of the closest security guard. "I'll just wait here. I've probably lost my touch while sitting out at Springdale." Things were going exactly as she intended them to go and it pleased her that she felt relief in knowing they would be caught.

Matt and Nicole entered the store and Nicole did as she always did when she and Matt worked as a team. She walked over to ask the clerk pointless questions while Matt went about the business of taking the shoes. Cory smiled when she saw Matt pick up the shoes and put them under his coat. As he lingered a minute before leaving the store, Cory walked up to the security guard and told him that the young man in the store had just stolen a pair of shoes and that the young girl with him had been part of the theft. Seconds after they left the store, the guard stopped Matt and Nicole. It was the first time that Matt had ever been caught stealing. His face showed his fear and his hands shook as Cory heard him trying to lie to the security guard. Cory could hear Nicole denying that she even knew Matt, but the guard ignored her. The revenge was made better by Cory quietly whispering to any who would listen that the young man and girl had been caught stealing. As the crowd that had gathered around Matt and Nicole grew larger, Cory's satisfaction increased. She felt a great sense of relief in knowing that some of her anger for the two of them fell away as she saw them marched off toward the security office.

On the bus ride back to the apartment Cory could not free her thoughts from what happened. She had wanted both Matt and Nicole to know the horrible feeling of what it was like to be betrayed. By the time she arrived home, the satisfaction from her revenge had begun to disappear and once again she felt empty and alone.

Margaret was in the kitchen preparing dinner when Cory walked through the door. "Oh, my God. I was so worried about you. I had no idea where you went. I was terrified that you had gone to the mall. You know that would have been against the rules. Where have you been, Cory? Why did you do this to me?"

"Mom, if you don't mind, stop always thinking about

what I'm doing to you and think once in a while what it is you're doing to me. Just once can't we have life center on me? Can you just once not be telling me about how hard you work, or how much worry I cause you, or about dad's problems? Just once I want the world to revolve around me and what's wrong in my life."

Despite the sympathy Margaret felt for Cory, it still frightened her that her daughter had so many angry feelings. "Cory, being young doesn't mean you are the only one with problems. Growing up is tough. I know that. Until you get some understanding of how tough it's going to be as an adult, you don't have any right to judge me or your father. I'll tell you again, and I'll keep telling you. We did the best that we could do."

"I doubt that."

"What would you have had us do, Cory?"

"You didn't have to get a divorce and move me around all the time. I don't have any friends. I don't belong any place. I'm just this kid who packs up every year and moves some place else. I hate moving. Don't you understand that? I hate moving and not feeling like I really live any place where anyone knows me."

"That's not true, Cory. We moved several times after the divorce, but we've been here for over a year. Surely in that time you could have made friends if you tried. You don't try. It's like your counselor said. You have this chip on your shoulder. I don't think you know what makes you angry. You just want to be angry. No matter what, you're going to find something to be angry about. If it's not me, it's going to be your father, and if it's not your father, it's going to be Rory. Something. Always something. It's you, Cory. It's not us. It's you." Margaret raised her voice and hit her hands against the wall. "Oh, Lord. This isn't the way I wanted your visit to be. It just isn't what I wanted."

"Me neither." Cory stood up and went to her room. "Tell Dad that I'm not going with him. I don't want to be around him or that kid of his." Cory slammed her door and lay down on the bed. Her only thoughts were about some type of harm coming to Rory. She was sure she was going to be sick to her stomach as one thought after another came to mind about Rory dying or being injured. What made the hideous thoughts even worse was that Cory felt pleasure over Rory being harmed.

Throughout the night Cory tossed and turned. In the morning Cory refused to leave her room until it was time to go back to the van. Martin did not need any lengthy conversation with Margaret to know that the visit had not gone well. Cory's face appeared vacant and empty. Margaret looked exhausted and almost relieved to be putting Cory back in the hands of Martin. Martin tried to make it easier by saying, "You should never expect very much from the first few visits. These kids have a lot of adjusting to do. Until they start talking about some of their feelings, they don't know what their feelings are. They get pretty mixed up."

"I guess I just hoped." Margaret tried to reach out and touch Cory, but she pulled away. "I wanted Cory to have a good time. Nothing worked out."

"You can count the times on one hand and have five fingers left over when it comes to things working out right the first few times they are home. You're not alone." Martin made no attempt to keep his words a secret from Cory. "Come on, young lady. Get your butt on the van."

Cory flashed him an angry look. "Don't call me young lady. I hate that."

Unlike Margaret, Martin did not take much from the young ones with whom he worked. "Better watch the mouth. You're heading back to some rules and regulations that you might have forgotten about."

Just as Martin was about to pull the van away from the curb he turned once more to look at Cory. He saw the same look of depression that he had seen so often on Cory's face when Cory first came to Springdale. Martin decided that he would have a conference with Mrs. Knight when he arrived back at Springdale. In the beginning Martin agreed with the others. They concluded that Cory would be one of the easy ones with whom they had to work because her problems were not nearly as severe or tragic as those of the other children. Looking at her face now, Martin knew they were wrong about Cory. Martin was sure he was right when he summed up Cory. She was only sixteen, but she was suffering from depression. Cory, he was positive, was going to withdraw again if they didn't help her. Martin sighed as he pulled the van away from the curb. Somehow he and the others at Springdale had to help Cory realize that she desperately needed help.

CHAPTER EIGHT

Sean waited outside the classroom door for Cory. He knew there was no way that she could have yet found out that it was Ginger who had been brought back to the infirmary. The residents all saw and heard the ambulance pulling into the driveway at Springdale, but most assumed that the ambulance had come to get Terrance rather than to bring Ginger back. Nearly three weeks had passed since the day when she ran away. Sean, like Cindy, was shocked when he saw Ginger lying in the bed. Her face was still bruised and her arm was in a cast. Except for Jeff and Cory, all the team had been to see Ginger and to offer their support. Winnie was so disturbed by Ginger's appearance he screamed out, "They ought to kill that no good father of hers. They ought to kill him. He's useless. They ought to kill him."

Martin sent Winnie back to the dorm with Sean. Then Sean went to tell Cory that Ginger wanted to see her. Martin arranged for Cory to have the afternoon off as he thought the best therapy for Ginger would be to sit and talk to the only one to whom she felt close.

The minute Cory saw Sean she guessed what it was. "It's Ginger, isn't it?"

"Yeah. She's the one they brought back in the ambulance." Sean tried to touch Cory's arm but she pulled away. "She looks pretty bad. That skunk of a father really hurt her this time. He beat her up and then her aunt tried to cover up what he had done by hiding Ginger from the authorities. It's been a bad three weeks for her. She wants to see you. Martin said you could stay as long as you like. You can even eat supper in the infirmary with Ginger. He says that maybe you can get her to eat something."

"Did they lie to us about not knowing where she was? I bet they lied to us. They knew all along that she was going to go to her father's and that he'd hurt her. I know they lied. They lie about everything."

"I don't think so, Cory. Mrs. Knight stormed out of the infirmary, and said she was going to see that an advocate pressed charges for Ginger. Mrs. Knight was really ticked off. I even saw her crying. I know no one wanted this to happen to Ginger even if she did run away."

Cory wondered why Sean trusted them all. Now because he trusted them, Cory no longer trusted him. As she walked toward the infirmary Cory felt the anxiety that seldom left her anymore. Ever since she had come back from her first home visit Cory recognized that the anxiousness was coming more often. What bothered her the most was she thought everyone was watching her and waiting for her to do something wrong so that she could be punished or lose privileges. Instead of talking more in group as she had started to do when she first arrived at Springdale, Cory now remained silent and suspicious of anyone who claimed to want to help her. "I'm glad Ginger wanted to see me. I'm the only one she can trust. No telling what medicine they're giving her. They're probably going to drug her."

"Honest to God, Cory, I don't know where you get so

many nutty ideas." Sean shook his head. "You think everyone is out to get you. I bet you anything that you even think that about me. You forget that I always stand up for you just like Ginger does. You know, Cory, everyone doesn't mean you harm. That's what Martin tries to tell you in group. One of these days you have to start looking at things the way they really are rather than the way you think they are."

Cory stopped and stamped her foot. "Don't start in about that paranoid stuff with me. Ever since you guys learned that word that's all you have to say to me. "Cory, don't be paranoid. Cory, quit acting paranoid." It's like you don't know any other word. You're not my friends even if you pretend like you are. Not one of you wants to be friends with me."

"Forget it, Cory. Just go on in and see what you can do to help Ginger. Please, though, don't get on her case about anything. She's got enough to deal with as it is."

"In other words, Mr. Know-it-all, I'm not supposed to go in and act *paranoid*. You think I'm some sort of stupid fool. I wouldn't do anything to hurt Ginger. Why can't you even trust me to help my friend?" Cory pushed the door open and entered the infirmary.

Except for Ginger, the room was empty. Ginger's face was turned toward the wall. When she heard the door, she turned toward the sound of the approaching steps. "Cory? Is that you, Cory?" Her voice was barely a whisper.

"Ginger!" Cory looked at the yellow bruises all over

Ginger's face. "Oh, Ginger, I'm so sorry." Cory leaned over the bed and kissed her friend. "Why did you run away? Things were going so well. You were on a team and everything. You just shouldn't have run away like you did. None of this would have happened if you hadn't run away."

"It was crazy wasn't it?" Ginger folded her fingers around Cory's. "I just had to tell him how I hated him. The more I thought about all that he had done to me, the more I wanted to tell him that I hated him. I'd never told him that. I told everyone else, but I never told him. Now he knows that I hate him and that I'll always hate him. Can you believe that it makes me feel better to know that he knows? Even though he beat me up, I feel good because I finally told him how I feel."

"Why didn't you just write your horrible father and tell him? You didn't have to run." Cory had no intention of saying a thing about the privileges that the team was likely to lose because of Ginger's having run. Cory's mind raced with all the things that she thought the counselors would do to them to make the next month miserable for everyone on the team.

"Are you worried that we'll all have to sit in the dayroom and that we won't get to see any movies or do anything like that? I mean do you think the team is going to get it because of my running?"

Cory avoided the question. "Forget that. No one cares. All we care about is you. We just all want you to get better."

"Mrs. Knight said that no one would be punished. She promised me that. I think she's really trying to be fair with me."

"That'll be the day. Like Mrs. Knight says, her lot in life isn't to make us happy. She doesn't care about us, Ginger. This is just a job for her."

Ginger shook her head. "I don't think so. I think they do care here. Who in their right mind would want to work with a bunch of delinquent kids if they didn't think they could do something to help them?"

Despite the pitiful appearance of Ginger and despite knowing that she still must be in pain, Cory was annoyed by her defense of the counselors and Mrs. Knight. "They're starting to brainwash you, Ginger. You're actually starting to believe them."

"Cory, don't you remember when I first came here how you told me to try? I hung in there because of what you said. Running away was a dumb thing to do, but after I realized how much I hated my father, I had to get to him and tell him that. Other than that stupid thing, I really have tried. One reason I tried was because of you. I felt like you believed in me. Now I don't think you believe in anyone. I'm not even sure you believe in me or our friendship. Do you, Cory? Do you believe I'm your friend?"

Until Ginger had defended the counselors and talked about the people at Springdale trying to help them, Cory believed that Ginger was a true friend. Now she looked at

Ginger's bruised face and wondered if she would keep their secrets or if she would turn on her in group as the others did. Rather than admit her doubts, Cory smiled and took Ginger's hand. "Of course I believe you, Ginger." With the lie came the anxiousness that never seemed to be absent from Cory's mind. "Do you want me to read to you? Maybe I could get some checkers and we could pass the time playing a game or two. Tell me what you want me to do to help you, Ginger."

"Just be with me. Sometimes just being with someone is the most important thing that you can do. I feel so alone right now. I just want to be with someone." Ginger held Cory's arm. Tears rolled down her cheek. "You know what I wonder about sometimes, Cory? I really wonder what it would be like to have a mother. I can't tell you how many times I've thought how different my life would have been if I just had a mother. What's it like to have a mom?" Ginger's eyes pleaded with Cory.

"It's not as great as you might think. I barely remember what my mom was like when I was younger. Now all it means is having someone crabbing at me. I never do anything right. She's always busy working or cleaning. You probably got some idea what moms are like from watching television. Moms aren't like the moms on television."

"Oh, I know that. I'm not that ignorant. I know life isn't like it is on TV."

"I don't even watch a lot of those shows anymore. I

134

mostly watch the videos because I don't want to see all that pretend baloney. Doesn't it make you sick how those characters in the television programs all got these neat families? No matter what kind of problem they got, it all gets worked out in about twenty minutes. They not only get their problems worked out, they get to wear these beautiful clothes for the show. They live in these nice houses and everything goes great at school. My life isn't like that, Ginger, and neither is yours. Have you ever seen any of those sitcoms and the father is beating up his daughter? Come on, get real. Have you ever seen anything like that? None of those kids go to school at places like Springdale. They have friends coming and going from their houses and their dads take a real interest in them." Cory was unaware that she was crying. "Our lives aren't like that. There's not a kid at Springdale who has a life like that. It isn't fair. Who wants to see all that garbage about nice families? I don't. I don't ever want to see that stuff."

"Cory." Ginger was pinching her friend's arm. "What's wrong, Cory? You're crying. They're just television shows. Like you said, they're all pretend. We all know they're pretend."

Cory's voice began to tremble. "Then why do they bother to show us that stuff. Don't they know that it hurts us to see those things? We're not normal and we don't like to be reminded that we're not normal. Darn, Ginger, don't you ever want to be normal like the kids on television?"

Ginger reached out and patted Cory's hand. "Calm

down, Cory. It's going to be okay." Ginger felt some
sense of disappointment because she had hoped Cory could
comfort her. In the end it was she who had to reach out and
help Cory. Then Ginger quickly felt relief. There was a
comfort in knowing that perhaps she had more strength
than she realized she had. What she had endured over the
last several weeks was far worse than what Cory had
experienced over the last three weeks, and yet, of the two
of them, Ginger was sure that she was the stronger.

As Ginger stared at Cory she tried to understand some
of the pain that her friend must be feeling. "Cory, it's all
right to admit you need help. I'm really beginning to see
that now. You have to reach out, Cory, and then they'll be
able to help you. All you have to do is say that you need
help."

"You're a fine one to talk. You didn't reach out. You
ran away."

"I admit it was among the dumbest things I've ever
done, but I just felt I had to do it. Once I left here I got
scared. I worried what would happen to me and the guys
on the team. Everything got all messed up in my head. I
kept hiding until I worked up the courage to go and see
him. The second I walked in his place I knew I had done a
very dangerous thing. After he hurt me I just didn't have
the courage to turn myself in. My aunt got scared that
something bad was going to happen to me. If she hadn't
been so scared that I might die or something, she'd never
have called the police.

"You know, Cory, once I was in the hospital and Mrs. Knight came to see me, I knew I was going to make it. I knew that somehow Springdale was going to help me. I couldn't wait to get back here. Especially to see you and Cindy and Sean and Jeff. I just know, Cory, if you and me are going to make it, we have to reach out and let them help us."

Cory shook her head. "You believe that. I don't." Cory twisted the piece of sheet that fell to her lap.

"What is it that you believe, Cory? I don't know anymore what you believe in."

"Me neither." A sense of sadness overwhelmed Cory. She wanted to believe in something and someone, but she could no longer trust the world or anyone in it.

CHAPTER NINE

Ginger sat down next to Cory on the floor of the recreation room. It was not often that all the residents were brought together at the same time. The bulletin that announced the gathering said only that there were to be guest speakers and the topic would be about developing survival skills.

The room hummed with the voices of the eighty residents who sat huddled together in small groups. Almost everyone sat with his or her team. Ginger and Cory did likewise. Ever since she had come back, Ginger's attitude toward Springdale and the other residents began changing. For the first time in her life Ginger thought of herself as a decent person who deserved good things to happen to her.

Mrs. Knight walked from the back of the room. As she passed each of the teams, her presence brought silence. By the time she reached the front of the room all conversation had stopped. "In two weeks we are going to start a program here that will involve you and inmates from the state prison. They are going to teach you how to camp." A hint of a smile crossed her face when she heard some of the residents laugh. She knew a few of them wanted to call out some insulting remark, but they restrained themselves because they knew such behavior could cost them points for the team.

"Believe me," she added, "this will not be any ordinary camping experience. In fact, I should be saying it will be a survival experience rather than a camping experience. If ever you needed to pay attention, it certainly will be when you begin receiving instructions. As to which team goes first, that will be decided by the draw of a number. If you draw a one, your team will go first. Like a lot of life, it's a matter of luck. With that said, I'd like to introduce Lester McAdams. Lester was sentenced to life imprisonment for the cold-blooded shooting of a cashier at a gas station. He has served seventeen years, which gives him a little background on prison routine. Isn't that right, Lester?" Mrs. Knight motioned to him. "Lester, may I introduce you to the residents of Springdale. Residents, this is Lester McAdams one of today's guest speakers."

Lester came from the back of the room. He was not a particularly big man, but there was something about the way he looked that was frightening. Every resident watched him walk down the aisle toward the front of the room. One of Jeff's legs hung over into the aisle. Lester paused a second and glared at Jeff. "Move it or I'll break it." He continued to move toward where Mrs. Knight stood. Jeff scooted away from the aisle so that he would not again be noticed. There was little doubt in Jeff's mind that the man with the scar down the side of his cheek could and would break his leg.

"I been on a tour of your cute little place." Lester laughed and stared until the residents dropped their eyes so that they wouldn't have to look at him. "Man, and you babies think you're locked up. You don't know the meaning of locked up." He cursed them, using obscene words that none of them had heard since arriving at Springdale. "You're at a Girl Scout camp here. Pink and blue isolation rooms. What a joke. You don't get it together, and you're going to be finding out about pitch black isolation, and they won't be bringing any salad and dessert on your trays. More than likely you're going to have to kill a few things on your plate before you start eating the garbage."

For the next hour Lester described life in prison. He told of the sexual assaults, the knifings in the food halls, the constant stealing that meant no one owned anything for very long, the prison doctor who sold drugs to the inmates in exchange for whatever the doctor demanded, the inmates who beat their heads on the floor as their sanity slipped away from months of isolation, the threats that went on night and day, the small cells filled with four too many inmates, and the knowledge that living with the brutality was not going to be measured in months, but in years. "That's my life. Forever until I die. I made dumb choices that carried me toward the taking of a human life. I didn't value my own life, and so I couldn't value anyone else's. I had to get to be thirty-five years old before I realized that I had a reason for living and that maybe I could do some-thing worthwhile with my life. That realization came in prison. It came after I had been beaten, threatened, trampled on, and assaulted. The realization didn't do me much good because for the next twenty, thirty, or forty years or however long I live, I'm going to continue to live with people who don't always respect human life.

"Get it together, you pigs." Lester thrust a fist at those who sat on the floor dazed by what they had heard him say. "While you're on vacation here at this fun and games place, you better do something about your lives. This isn't going to be what's it like behind the walls. There you'll learn about meanness. You'll learn about brutality. You'll be the victim or you'll be the one who is the attacker. I can't even tell which it is better to be. As the attacker you just get more mean and more brutal until you aren't fit to be around other people. Being the victim makes you so angry that you want to pay it all back and so you go out and commit more crimes. Then you get caught and you got to work it all out again. Are you going to be the victim or the attacker? It's a vicious circle. This place, me and the other cons want to try to help you break that cycle. You better listen because you aren't going to get too many chances."

After Lester finished speaking, a convict called Rower spoke. He was called Rower because he was always using a rowing machine to build up his muscles. Rower flexed his arms and the muscles bulged. "Who's gunna argue with me about whose turn it is to use the rowing machine? Yeah, we're all grown men and we fight over whose turn it is. Only difference between us and them kindergarten kids is we got knives and guns we made, and we got these." Rower again flexed his muscles. "You might think the guards and warden run the prisons to make sure we cons are doing what they're supposed to do. You're dead wrong. The inmates run the prison. Ain't that right,

Lester?"

"That's right. Now me and Rower want to introduce Charley. Charley's not a con. He took the right road. Charley get up here and tell them what's ahead."

A slightly built man joined the two convicts. "I'm Charley Fielding. My job is to get your team to where we're going. More importantly, I'm responsible for getting you back safely. I've been working with the survival training programs for about six years. Shortly after the programs were started, our director began involving prisons. In the last two years we've been going to centers such as this one and involving young people. The idea behind these programs is that if you can get through them, just about anything that you'll do in the future will seem easy by comparison. Believe me, you'll really get to know yourself and each other while we're out there."

Lester again spoke up. "We probably ought to mention again that very few detention centers are lucky enough to take part in a program like this one. If you want to be thankful about something, be thankful you got sent here to this little girl's place where all these counselors are looking after you. You got no idea what some of them other places are like. We've been to some of them and they are bad news."

Mrs. Knight stepped to where the three of them stood. "We've tried to impress our residents with the fact that the chances of juvenile offenders ending up in a place like Springdale are about one in ten thousand. Most of them complain about the facilities and how they've lost their rights. Trying to convince them that this a model facility that provides chances that most detention centers do not provide is a lost cause. If they're not willing to try to turn their lives around, our lecturing them on what's ahead is pointless. I appreciate your pointing out to them, Lester, that the treatment and help they get here is neither typical of most juvenile facilities nor like what awaits them should they choose to go on messing up their lives." Mrs. Knight glanced at her watch. "Maybe now we can move on to the survival experience that every resident at Springdale will have as a result of their being part of the program that the state is offering."

Lester felt insulted by her remarks. He narrowed his eyes and glared at Mrs. Knight. Her presence and his circumstances did not change who he was. "We'll move on when we're ready." Mrs. Knight turned to see the reaction of the residents. Most seemed stunned that she allowed him to speak to her in such a way. She said nothing as she let it sink in with them how powerful someone such as Lester could be. It was men like Lester, or his female equal, who were waiting for them if the young people could not be kept out of prison. She turned, sat down and reluctantly waited for him to begin when he was ready.

Lester leaned over and took a piece of paper from the table. He reached his hand out, and without saying a word, indicated that Mrs. Knight was to hand him a pen. "I want the leaders from every team up here." He stood tall as he

143

tore the paper in strips and wrote down as many numbers as there were teams. When the team leaders were in front of Lester, he shoved them in line. "Don't block my view of nothing. Draw a number." He held out the hand that contained the folded pieces of paper. "Who's got number one?" He almost snarled the question.

Marsha felt her knees shake. She was unable to answer him.

"Repeat. Who's got number one?"

Marsha raised her hand. Lester grabbed her elbow and yanked her out of line. "Lucky you." His smile looked evil. Lester's powerful hand remained wrapped around Marsha's arm. "Get the rest of your team up here." Then he cursed at the other residents as he ordered them out of the room.

Mrs. Knight had to remind herself that the program of putting hardened criminals together with youthful offenders had worked in other areas of the country. The whole idea of the program was for the young people to develop trust, and the irony was, Mrs. Knight didn't trust Lester. She knew, though, that with some of the youngsters she had to be willing to try new things if she hoped to help them. So far counseling and group sessions had not done much to change Cory and others like her. Their distrustful attitude toward other people remained the same. If anything, Cory and some of the others had become less trusting.

Mrs. Knight glanced over at Lester and wished she had a better source of help for the residents. The best that Mrs.

Knight could do was stand her ground when Lester asked her to leave. "I'm staying here." She returned the challenging look that Lester gave her. "I'm responsible for these youngsters." The thought of eventually having to turn her charges loose with the two convicts made her shudder, and it certainly made her question whether or not she had done the right thing when she agreed to become involved in the program.

Lester pointed to the floor. Cory and her team sat down, huddling together as if their closeness would protect them from Lester. "Starting bright and early on Saturday we're going to Arlen Forest. Our destination is Cree River. You're going to be carrying everything you need on your backs. If you're not in shape now, you will be by the time you see Springdale again. That's if you do." A slow grin spread across his face. He seemed to enjoy threatening them. "You'll survive if you trust us, and the news I got for you is you should never trust a con. We survive by lying and cheating and using brute strength. Puts you in a bit of a bind, right." He looked from face to face.

Jeff spoke out. "Suppose we don't want to go on this trip?"

"You'll go." Lester walked over to where Jeff sat. "You don't have any choice. Your team leader picked the right number. Believe me you're going to go."

"What if we get sick or something?" Jeff did not want to be in any forest or near any river with the man who stood hovering over him.

145

"It'll be tough on your team hauling along a sick punk so you better stay healthy. If you're too sick, you might not make it, and if you don't make it, they won't make it. Get my message, punk. You are all in this together." Lester moved away from them and motioned for Rower and Charley to come forward. "Charley and Rower are going to show you something. Then I want you to pick someone and you'll do it."

Rower stood a few feet in front of Charley. Charley put his arms out. Then he said, "Okay. Trust me." Rower tilted backwards and fell into Charley's waiting arms. Charley looked at Winnie. "Now pick someone and do it."

Winnie smiled and whispered to Gene. "If that's all we got to do, we don't have no problems." He stood up, pulling on Gene's arm. "You fall and I'll catch you."

Gene came around and stood in front of Winnie. Lester pushed Winnie farther back. Gene turned around to look at where Winnie now stood. Then Gene tilted his head back as if he intended to fall. He could not bring himself to fall backward into Winnie's arms.

"Hey, listen, Gene, I'm going to get you."

Gene turned his head again and again from the front of the room to where Winnie waited with his arms open. "Suppose you miss me."

"I'm not going to miss you for crying out loud."

"You could drop me."

Jeff spoke up. "Get going Gene."

Lester glared at Jeff. "Don't hassle him. Encourage

146

him, but don't hassle him or I'll kick some butt. Get what I mean." Lester waited for the others on the team to say something, but not one of them spoke up. He would not tell them to do what he knew they had to learn and that was to help each other.

Gene was taking quick, deep breaths as he grew more nervous. "If you think it's so easy, Winnie, you get around here and do it. I'll catch you."

"No problem." Winnie exchanged places with Gene. When he looked back at where Gene stood, the distance seemed farther away than when he had stood in back of Gene. Confidently Winnie turned around again and closed his eyes. He imagined himself falling backward. In his mind he didn't fall into Gene's arms. Instead he fell to the floor. "Are you going to catch me? Are you paying attention to what you're doing?"

"Yeah. Come on." Gene felt better now that Winnie was the one who had to believe that if he fell backwards his team mate would catch him.

Winnie sucked in a breath of air and arched his shoulders. Each time he tilted his head toward Gene he was sure that this would be the time that he could let his body fall into Gene's arms. On one try Winnie actually leaned so far that he lost his balance and fell to his knees as he fought to right himself. He looked at the others who sat watching him and Gene. "Believe me this isn't as easy as it looks."

Lester came over and pushed Winnie and Gene toward the other team members. "We can't keep this up all day.

Me and the boys got places to go and things to do. Your team better work on this and get it down pat so that everyone of you can fall backwards into the arms of someone you trust. Another thing I want you to do is blindfold each other. Each of you will have to depend entirely on the partner that sees. For at least a day, the only way you're not going to run into something or get bruised or fall in a hole is if you trust your seeing partner to guide you. And if you think this is a joke, you're mistaken. You better practice because you're going to need to trust someone before we get to Arlen Forest. You'll never make it up those mountains if you don't trust someone. Don't forget, you can't trust me and Rower. You can't trust cons. Charley is okay."

The suspicions that Mrs. Knight had about Lester eased somewhat. She was mature enough to see his purpose even if the young people couldn't. "I'll make sure that they get time to practice."

"You'll make sure of nothing. *They* better make sure they practice. It's up to them to figure out a solution to their problem. They aren't going to have any caretaker when they're trying to find a trail in the forest. They'll have to do some planning and some thinking or they'll end up going hungry. They don't need any nursemaid. They need to use their brains."

Mrs. Knight now realized there was a reason for everything Lester was saying and doing. The one thing that she kept wondering about was whether the young people could or couldn't trust him. She had her own doubts even though she had been reassured by all those who ran the survival program that Lester and Rower were among the best of the trainers. If she doubted the convicts after having been reassured that they would not allow anything to happen to the youngsters, she could only imagine how distrustful the youngsters themselves must feel. "They'll be ready on Saturday."

Cindy clutched Sean's arm as they left the room. "How could we have ever thought Mrs. Knight was mean? Compared to Lester, she's a saint. Gad! I'm not going any place with those horrible men. We'll end up cut to pieces in the forest."

Gene put his arm around Jeff's shoulder. "What did you think? Are those guys crazy or what? They were pushing Mrs. Knight around. Like not letting her say nothing. We got to get ourselves out of this."

Sean asked, "Where's this Arlen Forest?"

Cory spoke up. "I've been there."

The team stopped and gathered around Cory. Ginger held her friend's arm. "So what do you know about it?"

"It's been a long time since I've been there. I just remember there were picnic tables and swings where my Dad took me."

Jeff laughed. "So what's the big deal? It sounds like a place where kids play. We're probably making more out of this than we should. I know those geeks are trying to scare us to death. They can't let anything happen to us. The state isn't going to let us die or anything. The state could get in all kinds of trouble. Our story would be all over the newspaper."

"Yeah," said Winnie. "A newspaper story will do me a lot of good if I starve to death in a forest." He shook his head. "Go on, Cory. What else do you know about Arlen Forest?"

"There are some trails there. I know the trails go up to about three or four thousand feet. I've never been on them, but I heard other kids talk about them. Some of the kids at school have been there with the Scouts and stuff like that. I know the mountains aren't as bad as they are in some places, but they can get kind of steep. Canoeists use the river all the time. At least as far as Belton. After that the river gets pretty bad." Cory closed her eyes and shook her head. "I know they wouldn't take us to Belton. That's dangerous. They can't endanger our lives. I agree with Jeff. The state can't let anything happen to us. We're just kids."

Marsha corrected her. "Juvenile offenders. Who would care what happens to juvenile offenders?"

Sean put his hand up to stop all the conversation. "You know we can keep talking and talking about this, but the fact is, Mrs. Knight is sending us off with these crazy cons on Saturday. We're supposed to practice that falling and walking around blindfolded. I'd say we better figure out when we can do that what with us all having different school and work schedules."

"He's right." Ginger agreed with Sean. "So far we've only been told to do two things. We better do like they said."

"Why should we?" Gene challenged her. "That stupid moose said we couldn't trust him."

Ginger leaned against the wall. "I get the idea we got to trust each other. That's what he's asking us to do now. That includes you, too, Cory. You have to trust us."

"Just shut up, Ginger." Cory defended herself. She felt singled out by Ginger. "There's no law that says I have to trust any of you."

Even Sean lost patience with her. "This isn't going to be any play stuff, Cory. They didn't haul us in for that meeting for no reason. Those cons didn't give us their stories for no reason. That Lester didn't tell us to practice that falling and that walking around blindfolded for no reason. That warning Lester gave us about trusting each other wasn't given for no reason. He was making it clear to us that if we don't trust each other, we're all going to be in trouble."

Cory raised her voice when she answered him. "You can't help what you can't help." Cory started to walk away. Sean put his hand on her elbow.

"Somehow we have to start changing that, Cory." He looked so serious that all of them stopped talking. "Let's get back to setting a time for practicing the falls."

It took another fifteen minutes to work out a time and place for their first practice. Without anyone having chosen Sean, they all suddenly found themselves turning to Sean for answers. Whether he liked it or not, Sean somehow had emerged as a leader. After he had written down the time when they all would meet again, he ran to catch up with Cory. "I don't know what's going to happen, Cory, but I want you to know you can count on me."

"Another guy once told me that. I found out he lied. I found out I couldn't count on him for anything."

"I'm not that guy," Sean replied with confidence. "You can't blame me for what other people have done to you."

"You're not much different than other people. People are just people."

Sean shrugged his shoulders. "That doesn't make sense, Cory. If everyone were the same, we wouldn't be dealing with people like Lester and Mrs. Knight. They're sure not alike."

"I don't trust either one of them. So what's the difference to me."

"One's in prison and the other one is in charge of one."

"Stop with it. This isn't any prison."

"You know what I meant. You're like Gene. You're just ready to go off all the time. You didn't used to be that way. I think I liked you better when you were quiet."

"What you like doesn't matter to me." Cory realized she was doing the same thing to Sean that she did to her parents. The nicer they became, the more vicious she became. Cory wanted to test those who said they cared about her. If they could go on caring about her despite what she did, then Cory would believe they loved her. Sean, like her parents, had tried to tell Cory that he loved her. Once the words came out of his mouth, Cory began challenging him with bitterness and hateful remarks.

Sean put his hands in his pocket and lowered his head. "I was sort of hoping that what I liked might matter to you. I told you how I felt about you. Don't you believe what I'm saying?"

Cory shuddered as she remembered sitting on her father's lap and his saying the same thing. He told her how he loved her and how he would always be there for her. Cory found comfort in his gentle words. They were unlike the violent words that he screamed at Cory's mother. Even though she hated the screaming and the yelling that went on between her mother and her father, she was more saddened when they parted. When the fights were over, Cory's father would hold her and tell her that the yelling had nothing to do with anything that Cory had done. Sometimes it was her mother who first comforted her, assuring her that the problem was between the adults and that the problems were not caused by anything that Cory had done. Almost every time her father held her, he would say the same thing. No matter what happened between him and Cory's mother, he would always be there for Cory. Again and again he asked his child, "Don't you believe what I'm saying?" Then one day he was gone and Cory no longer believed anyone.

Now the question that Sean put to Cory frightened her. It was as if he had carefully chosen the words to mock her. "No, I don't believe what you're saying. I don't believe anyone."

"I don't know what's ahead for us at Arlen Forest, Cory, but I sure got the idea that you better start believing and trusting in someone or you're going to get us all in trouble."

CHAPTER TEN

Lester, Rower, and Charley were waiting for Marsha and her team. The girls didn't look any different than the boys as they approached the convicts and the guide who would be in charge of them for the next twelve days. Everyone on the team wore army fatigue pants with pockets along the sides, khaki T-shirts, and surplus army shirts that seemed far too hot for the unusually warm spring weather. They had on billed caps with a fine netting that could be pushed back under the bill. Although the young men found the clothes perfectly acceptable, none of the girls wanted to look at themselves in the mirror after they put on the clothes they had been given.

They all trouped aboard the van and waited for the three who would be their leaders. Mrs. Knight walked along with the leaders as they moved toward the young people. Mrs. Knight waited until Lester, Charley, and Rower had stepped into the van before speaking to the team. "I'd like all of you to make some notes about this experience. You're the first to do this. What you learn will be taught to the next team, and you'll be doing the teaching. How many problems you have will depend on how much help Lester and the others give to you. You can learn from their experience. In the future, how well the next team does will be up to your team because you're going to teach them what you find out. I wish you the best of luck, and I hope you all come back." With that comment, she smiled and nodded to Lester to close the van doors.

The team huddled together at the front of the van as most of the floor space was taken up with blankets, knapsacks and cardboard boxes. Jeff tried to peer into the boxes to see what they contained. Rower shoved him back. "You'll find out in good time what's in there." He winked at Lester. "Want me to get started?"

"Go for it."

"Okay, can the chatter and listen up. Here's what you got to decide first, and you got twenty minutes to decide." Rower held up a yellow slicker with a hood. "This here's a raincoat if you hadn't figured that out. Look carefully. I mean carefully." Rower continued holding it for another fifteen seconds. Then he folded up the slicker and put it back in a box. "This is your other choice." He unrolled a long sheet of clear plastic. "You can't take both with you because you're going to be carrying everything you need on your backs. In twenty minutes you all have to agree on your decision. Once you agree, you can't ever complain about the choice your team has made. If you can't agree to agree, none of you will take anything." Rower looked from face to face. "In twenty minutes you have to have a decision that's going to affect you for the next twelve days. Any questions?"

Like the others, Winnie sat in silence because he was unsure what it was he should be saying. "What's the big deal about a decision? If we take the slicker we can wear it instead of carrying it. That's one less thing to carry."

"Hold on," Sean cautioned. "I'll bet you they didn't

offer us a choice if the choice was all that easy. They're doing this to make us think. We haven't thought about anything so let's not jump in and decide right away on the slicker. What do you think, Cindy?"

"I haven't got a clue. I bet they are just trying to trick us into thinking we got a big decision. I sort of agree with Winnie. Let's take the slickers."

Sean shook his head. "I think the slicker weighs more than the sheet of plastic. He said we had to carry everything on our backs. That might mean we can't wear the slickers."

Cory agreed. "Did you see how Rower folded that plastic up? It was just this little pile when he finished folding it. Rower," Cory turned to the thin man in the back of the van and asked, "can we wear the slicker?"

"I asked if any of you had any questions. None of you did. Now it's too late for questions."

"For crying out loud," Gene complained. "How were we supposed to know we couldn't ask any questions later?"

"Now you know." Charley frowned.

"What we need to think about," Sean leaned toward the group, "is that the slicker and the plastic can both keep us dry. If we got to get in water, neither one is going to keep us dry. They can be used to keep us dry only if it's raining, and it can rain day or night. Now which one of them is likely to keep us dry whether it rains when we're up or when we're sleeping? That's what we need to think about."

"Did the slicker go to the knees or ankles?" Marsha squinted as she tried to recall the length of the yellow slicker. "Does anyone remember?"

For several minutes they discussed whether Rower had the slicker against him or if he had held it up by his head when he showed it to them. Not one in the group had the slightest idea as to the length of the slicker. Each recalled Rower telling them to look carefully, and each knew they had not observed what would now help them to make a better decision.

"Could I butt in and remind you that we're running out of time?" Gene rapped his knuckles against the metal roof. "Besides, what does it matter how long the darn thing is. Just pick something and let's forget all the discussion?"

"It does matter," Sean corrected Gene. "If the slicker is too short, it won't cover our feet when we're trying to sleep."

Suddenly the meaning of Sean's comment dawned on Marsha. "You mean to tell me we're going to sleep outside?"

"Think about it." Sean looked from one to the other. "I sure don't see any tents any place in this van. And you can bet they wouldn't be talking about learning survival skills if they were taking us to a cabin in the forest. Did you think we were all going to the Holiday Inn, Marsha?"

"I didn't think about it, either." Cory sympathized with Marsha. "How could we have not thought about it? We were stupid."

"Don't count me as stupid." Sean smiled. "It never occurred to me but what we'd be sleeping outside. I've slept outside plenty of times. Not in the woods, of course. It can't be any more dangerous out there than it was in some of the places I've slept."

"I'll go along with that," Ginger agreed. "When I ran away from home I slept in cars and fields and all kinds of places. There were crazies all around me. At least the animals don't have knives and guns."

"Animals!" Marsha shuddered. "What kind of animals?"

"Let's talk about that stuff later. If we don't make up our minds, we're not going to get the slicker or the plastic." Sean turned their attention back to the problem at hand. "We don't know whether or not they are going to let us wear the slicker. The plastic would be easier to carry. We can cut a hole in it and wear it if it comes to that. We can sleep on it to keep from getting cold. We can cover up with it to keep from getting wet. I know for a fact it's got to be longer than the slicker because I remember it dragging on the floor when Rower was rolling it back up. My gut feeling is we could do more with a sheet of plastic than we could do with a slicker. Anyone else got any other suggestions?"

Gene asked, "And how did you get in charge of this is what I'd like to know?" Gene resented the fact that everyone seemed to be listening to Sean. "I don't know as how we put you in charge of anything."

159

Ginger pointed her finger at Gene. "So what are you complaining about? You got a better suggestion or something? Sean's using his brain. That's what Lester told us to do. All you want to do, Gene, is run your mouth. Sean's trying to come up with some sensible solutions so shut up."

"We better cut this out." Cindy told them what she thought. "I say we go along with Sean. Let's vote. How many say we take the sheet of plastic instead of the slicker?"

Everyone but Gene raised a hand. "When we wish we had taken the slicker, I don't want anyone blaming me for taking that stupid sheet of plastic."

Rower interrupted them. "We told you the decision had to be unanimous. You're going to have to keep talking until you all agree."

All of them turned on Gene. Jeff finally spoke up. "You better agree, Gene, because we don't want to mess around with you."

Gene crossed his arms in front of him. "Rower said we had to agree. You guys are threatening me. That's not right."

"Vote, Gene." Winnie leered at Gene. "Vote, and you better vote our way. Do you want to count us again, Rower?"

This time Gene barely put his hand up to signal he agreed with the others. "I can see how we're really going to help each other. Man, I can really see that. I don't trust any of you."

Cory leaned her head back. She hated the word *trust*. For weeks that was all the counselors and Mrs. Knight kept talking about. Her stomach ached every time she thought that for the next twelve days she would come up against that word again and again. Even after they had made their decision to take the plastic, she was not sure if she could believe or accept the reasoning of the others. Not only did she not trust them, she didn't trust herself.

The van stopped at a clearing near the edge of a farm. "We're getting out here to relieve ourselves and to fix lunch." Charley spoke quietly. The team followed their leaders to a grove of trees. "The toilets are over there." Charley pointed to a clump of bushes.

The girls looked at each other. Marsha had a puzzled look on her face. "You mean we're going to have to pee and stuff in bushes?"

Sean laughed. "You sure don't have much of a handle on camping."

Rower grunted. "You guys need to get it in your head that you aren't camping. You're surviving. This part is easy. You wait until you get to the hard part."

Each of the girls took a turn marching up the little hill to the bushes. Lester quickly silenced the boys when they made remarks about the girls. "There isn't any difference in the sexes here. We're all just survivors. Everyone has to go. That's a natural part of living so shut your mouths and stop with those stupid comments."

Marsha whispered to Cory. "Could you go?"

"I had to go real bad so I went."

"I couldn't do it. What do you think will happen to me if I can't go the whole time we're gone?"

"Come on, Marsha. Don't be silly. You'll get used to it."

"But what if I don't. I could just blow up."

"I don't think anyone has ever blown up from not going to the toilet."

"This isn't going to the toilet. This is going to the bushes."

Lester heard what the girls said. "You better work at it, Marsha, or you're going to end up with stomach cramps."

Marsha blushed at the thought of her toilet habits being discussed out loud. "I wish you would all be quiet about me and the bushes."

Charley hauled out ropes from the van. "Get your lunch down and then you're going to learn something about these ropes."

The team sat on the ground eating sandwiches. Cindy gave her sandwich to Jeff because she didn't like the lunch meat. Rower warned her that she better eat what was put in front of her. "Compared to what's coming, that lunch meat will taste pretty good."

Cindy picked up the orange and peeled it. "I don't care how hungry I get, I'm not eating anything I don't like."

"Have it your way." Rower shrugged his shoulders. "Before this is all over, all you guys are going to learn that you better listen to what we say."

162

Charley asked them to move in closer to where he had the ropes laying on the ground. "Sean, Jeff, and Cory, get up front here. I'm going to show you how to put these ropes around your waists. There are going to be some times when the only thing that will keep you from falling down something, into something or over something is the fact that you'll be attached to someone else who will have a firm grasp on a tree, a rock, or something that will keep you and them from killing yourselves." Charley began with Jeff. He tied the rope around his waist, leaving several feet of rope between him and Sean. Then he wrapped the rope around Cory. "Did you all see how that was done?" He looked at their puzzled faces. "Okay. We'll do it again."

Rower grabbed Winnie. "Get up there and do what Charley did. Marsha, Cindy, and Gene, now it's your turn with Winnie. The rest of you get that rope off you and keep practicing until it goes around you just like Charley had it."

For the rest of the afternoon the team tied ropes, wrapped ropes, and undid ropes until their hands were red and sore from the ropes being drawn through their palms. "You got to toughen up," Lester warned them. "Don't let those ropes drag through your hands or you'll get rope burns." He seemed not the least sympathetic to the red blisters each of them had on their hands. "Tomorrow you'll wear gloves so that your hands get a break."

Late in the afternoon they loaded up the van and left the grove. Lester looked at their tired faces. "Don't get any ideas about going to bed early. We're going to practice some falling tonight and some walking around in the dark."

As they drove deeper along the winding road into the forest they passed a few campers. Before long there were no other people to be seen. The hum of insects was all that broke the silence of the forest. At the foot of the low-level mountains they could see the river. The river moved faster as it narrowed higher up in the mountains. Cindy looked out the window and over the side of the mountain. "I don't know about you guys, but it looks scary to me."

Supper consisted of dried beef, dried apricots and juice. "Enjoy that juice," Charley advised them. "Beginning at breakfast there will be only water. Water is going to be it until we get back. And you better watch how much water you drink because when we're out, we're out. Which brings us to your next decision. You need to think about whether each of you pays for your own mistakes, or is the mistake going to be shared by all of you."

Ginger spoke up. "Can we ask questions now?"

"Yeah." Charley didn't smile as he wanted to. He saw that it only took one time and they had learned.

"What kind of mistakes are you talking about?"

"Food and water for a start. You've been warned that both have to be rationed or neither will last. You're going to be hungry and thirsty, but you better think about tomorrow and the next day. You can't live for the moment. Suppose some fool is looking after number one and he or she drinks or eats more than was allotted. If that person runs out of food or water, is that his or her problem or is it the problem of all of you?"

Jeff shook his head. "No way am I going to pay for someone else's mistake. If I'm thinking and planning so I don't go hungry or get thirsty, I'm not doing without because some clown like Gene ate all his food."

"What are you picking on me for? I ain't done nothing yet." Gene was annoyed that Jeff had singled him out.

"You will. You can bet on it." Jeff looked at the others to see if they agreed. "What do you guys think?"

"There's a problem, though." Sean gave his opinion. "They told us that none of us could do this alone. We all have to survive or none of us survive. How are we going to survive if Gene is starving or doesn't have any water to drink? I been out on those streets between shelters or waiting on my mother to get out of one. Believe me, I know what it's like to be hungry. You can't walk very far when you're hungry."

Lester eyed Sean. Of all of them, Lester believed Sean not only thought more clearly, but his experience of surviving on the streets without help put him in a better position to survive in the wilderness. "I'll only say that Sean has a point. The decision is yours, though." Lester knew that in the end the only one who was likely to do something really stupid was Gene. He probably was the only one who would be selfish enough to let someone else go hungry or thirsty.

Cory thought how empty her stomach already felt and

165

this was only the first day. "Let's just agree that none of us should eat or drink more than we're supposed to. If we all agree, there shouldn't be any problem."

"That sounds fine," Winnie said, "but will we all do it?" He stared at Gene. Like Lester, Winnie believed it would be Gene who wouldn't do what he was supposed to do.

Sean once again took control. "We can't get away from the fact that we *all* have to get back. Since we all got to get back, we're going to have to share what we got and hope that no one screws us up. Will you all agree not to eat more or drink more than the day's rations?"

They all nodded. Ginger made one more request. "I think we should all hold hands and swear that we're not going to do anything that makes it hard on everyone else." Ginger thought about how she had seen mountain climbers in a movie make a pact. "Making a pact will help us to remember. We can remind each other that we made a pact. What do you say?" She stretched out her hands to the others. They all joined hands. "Close your eyes so that you act like you really mean it. Now I'll say what we got to remember and you repeat it. Okay?" Ginger closed her own eyes and began. "This team promises to do everything that is right and fair so that we all make it back." She waited for them to repeat what she had said. Then she went on. "No matter what, we will help each other so that we all succeed."

Cindy squeezed Ginger's hand. "That was very good. You know what? We might make it even if those darn drop-offs seem scary."

"I guess our decision is made, Lester." Sean spoke for the group. "We'll all pay if anyone makes a mistake."

No one on the team said anything else about the decision. They sat on a carpet of pine needles as it grew darker and darker in the forest. Rower explained to them what they would do for the next two hours. "I'm going to lead one of you for about fifteen minutes. You will put your hand on my shoulder and follow me. No matter what you hear, think, or feel, you are to keep your hand on my shoulder and trust me to guide you to safety. I will lead you back. Then the next one will do the same thing. You'll have your hand on my shoulder and someone else from the team will have his or her hand on your shoulder. Before it's all over, everyone of you will have to trust the one in front of you. Now do I have any volunteers?"

The only one who raised a hand was Sean. Lester was happy that his judgment of Sean had been correct. It made him feel better to know that his ability to size up people had not left him. He had not doubted that out of the group, Sean was the natural born leader. Lester guessed that the next to volunteer would be Ginger who had spunk and a wonderful sense of trust of those who treated her fairly. When Lester returned with Sean, the young boy was grinning. "That was quite a trip." It was so pitch black no one could see Rower and Sean standing above the group. "So who is it going to be that trusts me?"

As the leaders expected, it was Ginger who said, "I

want to go now." Lester knew it wouldn't be Marsha or Cindy because both were terrified of their surroundings. They would have to be coaxed to leave the spot where they sat huddled together on the ground. Jeff would willingly follow Ginger as he would assume if a girl could make it, he could make it. Winnie and Gene would argue about following Jeff because neither would want to be the last male to go. Cory would be the last one because she trusted the least. Lester knew Cory would hesitate and falter with every step never trusting the one in front of her.

The choices to follow along through the forest and to the edge of the river were as the leaders predicted. Charley nudged Lester as both stared into the blackness at the figures stumbling through the woods. "One hundred percent," Charley whispered to Lester. "We had them figured out one hundred percent."

"Yeah. We're getting pretty good at this," Lester smiled. We need to keep an eye on Cory. It's probably going to be Gene who deliberately does something stupid so we know we have to watch him, but Cory could get us in just as much trouble. It's going to be a battle getting her to trust us."

"We'll talk about it later." Charley believed Lester was right. He moved his hands along the trees, knowing even by the touch of the bark how far they had traveled. "You're doing fine, Cory. Keep that hand on Cindy's shoulder. Cindy is doing fine. If she's making it, you'll make it."

Cory dug her fingers into Cindy's back and shuffled along. Each step was an agonizing one for Cory. Cindy, still unsure of herself after having made the trip only one time, offered very little encouragement to Cory. The words of encouragement came from Sean and Ginger who by now had made the trip five times. There was nothing along the trail that frightened them any more. They not only believed in Rower who led them, but they believed in themselves.

"You're doing fine, Cory." Ginger called back even though she couldn't see her friend in the dark. "You're going to hear the river in a minute. It sounds worse than it is. The sound will come from below. You might feel like you're going to fall off the edge, but trust Cindy. You're not anywhere near the edge. It just sounds that way. Isn't that right, Sean?"

His voice sounded so far away despite the fact that he was no more than a few feet ahead of Cory. "Don't be frightened, Cory. You neither Cindy. You made it once, Cindy, so you can make it again. Just put one foot in front of the other and you'll make it no matter how terrible the river sounds. You're not going to be anywhere near the river."

The words of encouragement kept coming until suddenly Cory heard the river below. The water roared over rocks. Cory stopped. She could not make herself move. "I don't want to go any farther." Cory screamed at them. She took her hand from Cindy's shoulder and twisted around to run. Cory crashed into a thicket of trees and fell down.

Frantically she waved her arms and tried to stumble away from the branches that were scraping her legs through the long pants.

"Don't move," Lester calmly called out to her. "Cory, if you move away, you'll go deeper into the forest. It's pitch black, we won't be able to find you." Lester did what he hoped he wouldn't have to do. He flashed his light toward the direction of her voice. "Follow the light, Cory. Just follow the beam of the light."

"No. You'll make me go back by the river." Cory backed up until she stumbled over a fallen tree. "Don't make me go back by the river." She cried out the words.

Lester knew that if he gave in now, Cory would continue to be frightened. Everything that scared her or that involved showing that she trusted them would be the same. She would run from everything. "I'm not promising you that you won't have to follow the path again. That's part of the training. I am promising you that you'll be lost among those trees and have to spend the night by yourself if you take one more step away from us."

"Cory," Sean held his ground and called out. He understood that if he broke from the group, they all could get lost in the woods. "Cory, do as Lester says. We're not going to let anything happen to you."

Gene's knees shook when he realized that Cory was endangering them all. He did not sympathize with her. He felt only anger. "You're stupid, Cory. None of us can see. We're all scared and can get lost because of you."

Sean again called out. "Shut up, Gene. She's not stupid. She's scared."

"And what do you think I am?" Gene held even more tightly to Jeff's shoulder. "Get us out of this mess, Lester. Make her come back before we all get killed."

"No one is going to get killed, Gene. Be quiet now." Lester turned toward the direction of the flashlight beam. "Cory, Gene's right. You are endangering us. One of us will have to leave the group to come after you. They'll all have to stand here and wait until you can be located. It could be a lot simpler if you'd come to us. You can hear us and you can follow the beam. Not one of us can see you. You would do the right and the fair thing if you do what needs to be done. Please, Cory, cooperate."

All of them could hear the sound of Cory's feet crunching on the forest floor. Weakly she answered, "I'm trying to move toward the light, but I'm confused."

"Stop then. Get your bearings before you move again." Charley stood beside the others as he wanted them to know he was nearby. "Take a step and see if it brings you closer to the light. If it doesn't, wait a second and think which way you have to go to get closer to the light." Charley's voice tried to calm her because he knew she wasn't thinking clearly. There had been others before Cory and there would be others after her who in one way or another would go through some stage of panic before the course was over. Charley was aware that the longer Cory stood still or moved toward the light, the closer they would be to getting her back without any of them having to go after her. "Just move toward the light."

Suddenly they all saw her leg pass in front of the beam. "I'm sorry." Cory blurted out her apology and started crying. "You all hate me."

Only Sean and Ginger denied what Cory said. The rest of the team was angry with her for what she had done. Gene expressed how he felt when he called out, "They should have left you in the woods. Next time I hope they do."

Lester took Cory's hand. "I know you'd all like to call it a night, but it's not going down that way. Cory, you got to go through with what you started."

"Please don't make me do this. Please." Cory stepped back. Lester reached for her arm and pulled her toward him.

Sean asked Charley if he could go to Cory. Charley shook his head. "You have to learn to trust a lot of people in life, Sean. She might trust you and follow along because you're in front of her, but we can't always pick and choose who'll be in front of us. Cory has to trust Cindy."

The thing that Sean wanted to tell Cory was that he loved and cared about her. In the dark forest all he could manage was, "Cory, please do it. It matters to me that you make it."

His words did little to encourage her as she was too frightened. She let Lester place her hands on Cindy's shoulder. Cindy turned around. "We all made it, Cory, and you will, too."

The line once again started winding along through the trees toward the roar of the river. Cindy again felt Cory's fingers digging into her back. "Please don't pinch me so hard, Cory. It hurts."

The sound of the river grew louder as Cory blindly followed along. She made herself think about being back at Springdale safe in the dorm just as she used to imagine herself in her room at the apartment. One foot moved. Then the other and all the time she blocked out the night sounds of the forest and the thundering water below. Lester and Rower urged her to keep going, but the others remained silent, fearing they might say the wrong thing and cause Cory to panic again. Then Cory noticed that the noise of the churning water was beginning to lessen. She sensed if the sound was less, then they must be moving away from it.

"Are we heading back?" She barely whispered the words and feared the answer.

Lester patted her on the shoulder. "It's only a few yards and we'll be back where we started. You made it, Cory."

When they all realized that their ordeal was coming to an end, they cheered. Most of them simply fell to the ground and wrapped their blankets around their exhausted bodies. They were too tired to talk. Sean came over to Cory and knelt down. "Did you hear what I said out there?"

Cory nodded and pulled her blanket up to her neck. "I was such a baby. I know I made them all mad at me."

"Never mind about that. Did you hear what I said?"

"Yes."

"I mean it, Cory. I really care about you. There sure haven't been many people in my life that I ever cared about. You got to understand that you do matter to me. You just got to believe me and trust me."

"I'm not sure that I can." She wished it were not so dark as she wanted to see his face. "I trusted Matt and he not only made a fool out of me, he hurt me. I trusted my dad and he left me. Why should I trust anyone?"

"I'm not your dad and I'm not Matt. I'm me. Give *me* a break, Cory. I'm not to blame for what they did."

"Why does it matter to you what happens to me? Like how come when I was so scared you yelled out that it mattered to you what happened to me? What's so special about me?"

Sean didn't know why he felt the way he did about Cory. There was something about her that made him want to protect her. More than that, he wanted her to trust him. "I really don't know, Cory. From the first time I talked to you in class I thought there was something different about you."

"You've probably had a lot of girls you cared about." Cory's eyes were blinking shut. She wanted to go on talking to him, but she was too tired.

"Not really. I've moved around so much I never got to

174

know any girl." In the moonlight he could see that she was falling asleep. "Goodnight, Cory."

CHAPTER ELEVEN

On the fourth day out no one talked as much as they had the previous three days. The leaders gave them very little advice, preferring instead to let them think things through and come up with their own solutions. It was Jeff who suggested they repack the knapsacks so that some were lighter in weight than the others. When they started out, each one on the team carried a pack that weighed the same as everyone else's. Jeff reasoned that if they repacked their knapsacks, making some of them lighter in weight, then for at least part of the day they could take turns carrying less. The girls had more difficulty carrying the heavier packs. Marsha started out complaining, but when she found no one listened to her, she soon stopped. The girls learned to walk along as partners with one of them now and then pushing up the pack from the bottom so as to ease the weight away from her partner's shoulder.

The thing that bothered them the most was being thirsty. Talking about wanting more water only made it worse. Winnie wiped his forehead on his sleeve and looked up at the tall trees that shaded the path ahead. "Thank goodness for the trees. You know I swear I'm never going to pass a drinking fountain without taking a drink."

Gene licked his lips. "Can't you just see one of those drinking fountains that's all sweaty because the water is so cold? I'd give anything just to stand at one of those fountains and gulp down water."

"Will you guys shut up?" Jeff turned and glared at them. "We got a couple of hours to go before we get a great, big, generous couple of swallows of water. The last thing I want to be hearing about is ice water coming out of a fountain. Oh, God! Thinking about it is running me nuts."

At the top of the long path leading up the mountain Lester signaled them to stop and rest. "Rest." He slipped his pack off his back and looked at the group. All of them, including Gene, were doing much better than he or the other leaders had expected. They accepted sleeping on the ground, they had learned to use the ropes for climbing and repelling up some steep drop offs, they ate the dried food without complaining, and they had made some good decisions as to how they could best help each other. Cory still remained the one who had to be coaxed into doing anything. Long after the rest of them had made it up a hill or along a darkened path, one or the other of them had to persuade Cory to take the next step or to reach her hand out and take the hand of the person in front of her.

Instead of losing patience with Cory as they had in the beginning, they all became more patient. They wanted to pass onto to her the skills and confidence that they had gained. Cory was not yet ready to listen. Tomorrow would be the most difficult of tests. They would have to repel down a steep slope and forge the river. Cory would not make it if she wouldn't put her trust in others.

That night they sat in a small circle and again planned

out their food for the remainder of the trip. They all knew just how much food they could consume in one day. After tomorrow they would have come halfway. Winnie favored some type of celebration after they had forged the river. "Let's treat ourselves tomorrow night. Maybe a little extra water and a whole bag of dried apricots. Something sort of special."

It was always Sean who saw the possibilities of problems coming up. "You know I did that a couple of times. I had what I thought was plenty of food because I'd heard about some shelter that would take me in or I figured some kind of help was on the way. I stuffed my food into my mouth just sure there would be more where it came from. I was wrong. It's hell going hungry. We can celebrate when we get back. Then there will be plenty to celebrate. Anything can happen between now and the time we get back to the van. Anyone else agree with me?"

They all agreed with Sean. After five days out, they knew he was the one who thought the most clearly. Ginger spoke up and said that. "You've gotten us out of several messes. In fact, you're more help then they are." She pointed to Lester, Charley, and Rower. Then she laughed. "No harm meant, Wonderful Leaders. But when it comes to solving problems, I'll put my money on Sean. Sean ought to be a leader himself."

Sean's face turned red. He was grateful for the dark and the fact that no one could see how embarrassed he was. "I sure never thought I'd be a leader of anything. I sort of always thought of myself as a goof-off."

Gene disagreed. "You! I get the honors for that one." Gene drew circles on the ground with the branch that he held. "You know sometimes I didn't figure there was any purpose for me. I didn't like all that crap I was doing, but I couldn't think of anything else to do with my time."

"I was sort of that way myself," Marsha added. "I just hated what my stepfather did to me. When my mother didn't believe me, I just didn't care what I did just so long as I could get back at them."

"Getting back doesn't always work out." Ginger almost whispered the words. "I thought I'd feel better if I told my father what a rotten person he was. Yeah, I sure showed him. My back is still sore from the beating. I just don't see why parents have to be so darn mean to their own kids."

Cory felt the need to take part in what they were saying. Suddenly she didn't want them to think that every parent was as bad as Marsha's or Ginger's. "My parents weren't mean to me. They never beat me or anything like that. They just did some things that hurt me."

"Then how come you hate them?" Sean was pleased that Cory finally chose to volunteer information.

"I never said I hated them."

"You act like you do."

"I hate some of the things they did. Mainly my dad. He just left and he lied to me. He said he'd always be there for me, and he wasn't. If you can't believe your own

179

parents, who can you believe?"

"Me." Sean smiled. "I mean what I say."

"You know," Cindy spoke up, "I'm not sure which of us has got it worse. Some of us have been hurt and harmed by our own parents. I went hungry plenty of times because my mom was always running off some place. Sean walks the streets looking for a place to live. I don't get it. How come things are so hard for us and so easy for other kids? Did any of you ever wonder why there are plenty of kids at school and they seem to have everything? They come from nice homes and they got these normal parents. I hated going to school and looking at those kids."

"My life wasn't all that bad," Cory offered. "You know compared to all of you, I had things pretty easy and I still felt left out at school. Like I never belonged with any of the groups. With you guys I sort of fit in. We're all misfits. I know that. It kind of bothers me that I fit in with misfits. That's probably why no one at school liked me very much. I tried to blame them, but it must have been me." Tears fell down Cory's cheeks. "It wasn't like I didn't want to belong. It was more like no one ever asked me to belong and I didn't feel good enough about myself to ask them if I could be part of their group. I hate groups. Groups mean someone has to get left out."

Gene reached over and touched Cory's arm. "It's okay if you cry, Cory. I know just how you feel. My old drunken dad used to come to school. I couldn't help that my old man drank and smelled. The other guys made fun of me. I'd just want to strike out at those stupid guys. A couple of times I did. Then I got expelled for causing trouble. The good students ignored me. Not that I was a good student or nothing. I couldn't be a good student if I tried. The ones who were always in trouble ridiculed me. So who was I supposed to hang out with?"

"Part of the problem was not having any decent clothes." Sean's voice broke. "I not only didn't have any decent clothes, the ones I had smelled. I wasn't about to go to school. I just felt different than anyone else. It was easier to roam the streets and steal the stuff that I needed than it was to go to school."

"That's what I mean." Ginger's voice sounded angry. "Why should all that crap happen to us? We didn't do anything. How come someone nice like Sean has to live out on the streets and steal to keep alive? What about it, Charley? You're an adult. Maybe you got some answers. Why do I end up with a father that beats me and some other kid gets a father who buys her prom dresses? Come on and tell us why we should be good when nothing good ever happens to us."

Charley had been touched by their discussion. "That's like asking me why a four-year-old gets leukemia. The little kid has never smoked or drank or done anything wrong so why is the little kid hit with cancer. There are plenty of things that even intelligent, well-educated adults don't understand. No one will ever understand why things aren't fair in life. About all anyone can do is ask himself what's the best I can make of this situation. What do you think, Lester? You got any answers?"

Lester scooted in closer to the group. "Somebody asking me? That's crazy. I did more to screw up my own life than just about anybody I know. As bad as things were, I had no right to do what I did. We all got to pay for our mistakes. We're all out here trying to make sure you guys don't make any mistakes like me and them other cons. I know there are plenty of times you guys think I'm just running my mouth to hear myself talk. Ain't so. Prison is not a place anyone wants to be in." He lowered his voice and stared into the darkness. "Life. I'll be there for life. That's a tough thought to wake up with every single day. About all that keeps me going is these here courses. Somehow and in someway I got to know that I'm going to make a difference in someone's life. That someone is going to stay out of prison because of me.

"I been sitting here listening to you all talk," Lester continued. "You got every right to ask why life is dumping on you. I don't have any answers. About all I know is that you all already come through some bad times. You sure don't want to turn bad times into worse times. One way or another, you got to see the light while you're at Springdale. Learn everything you can and take that learning back to the streets with you. Survive not because of what happened to you, but in spite of what happened to you."

Winnie listened to every word that Lester said. The young boy was not unlike the others in that he wanted things to change in his life. "Is it true about the foster homes? At Springdale I keep hearing that some of the kids are going to foster homes."

"Yeah," Sean piped in. "We heard that the counselors and Mrs. Knight try to find foster homes for us. I don't know that I want to live in any foster home. I'd rather be out on the streets."

"Sure," Lester laughed. "Those streets are just the best place to get educated or to get some kind of job training. Educated in crap and trained in crime."

Gene wanted answers to his own questions. "I heard that some of those foster homes are pretty bad. Kids get abused just like Ginger and Marsha. Nobody listens to the kids and the foster parents lie because they want the money. Come on, Lester, level with us."

"Wait a minute." Charley took control of the group. "There probably are some foster homes that are worse than any of the homes that you people know about. But you got a right to speak up. If anything wrong is happening at a foster home, then you keep telling someone until someone believes you. There's no reason why you have to put up with abuse."

"Are you defending the foster homes?" Sean asked.

"I was raised in two foster homes." Charley spoke directly to Sean. "I hated the first one. The old man in that one had more problems than my own father. It wasn't any official foster home. This family took me in after my mother died. It was just some family in the neighborhood.

You probably couldn't get away with something like that now. I stayed with them nearly a year. I had enough sense to know that those people were nuts. They had me shoplifting and then moving on to bigger and better stuff. That old man never worked a day in his life. He lived off what his so-called foster kids stole.

"You're probably not going to believe this, but I got so desperate and was so afraid of getting in serious trouble that I just walked up to this cop one day and told him all about those people. Nothing could ever be proved against them, but the state got me and two other boys out from under their control. I ended up in another foster home. The McKendrees were the nicest people you'd ever want to know. I think of them as my mom and dad. There's no telling what would have happened to me if it hadn't been for them. I finished high school and got myself a decent job. About six years ago I decided that before I married Ellen and settled down, I was going to do something to help someone else. I was sort of given a break and I thought someone else needed a break."

"Big break," Gene moaned. "You pay back kids by torturing them to death, starving them, and all but pushing them off the side of the mountains. Let's give old Charley a hand, guys."

They all laughed at Gene's teasing. Despite all that had happened to them on the course, they knew that they were learning from the leaders and from each other. The most important thing they had learned was that they could do things they never dreamed they could do.

"Yeah. And you guys haven't seen nothing yet." Charley slapped his cap on Marsha's arm. "As for you, I'm just glad to see you finally learned how to use the bushes. I was afraid you were going to explode before you..."

"Shut up, Charley." Marsha screamed. Then she laughed as she recalled the afternoon when she sat behind a clump of trees and the others cheered her on until she had been able to relieve herself. "I don't want to hear anything more from anyone about my toilet habits."

Gene stood up and imitated how Marsha walked stooped over and hugging her stomach for several days as she complained that she would never be able to use a bush for a toilet. "Marsha's just a happy camper now. Right?" The group clapped for Marsha. "Let's get serious here." Gene sat down again. "Tell us some more about these foster homes. I'm like Sean. I know what I got with my father and his bottle. I don't know what's ahead in any foster home."

Cindy scoffed at Gene. "So who does know what's ahead! Do you want Charley to tell you how you're going to live happily ever after with some family like he had? Baloney. I learned the hard way that there aren't any guarantees. Nobody ever guaranteed me that I was going to have a place to stay and something to eat."

"So do you want to go to a foster home?" Sean asked.

"I don't know what I want." Cindy stared down at the ground. "I just know I'm too young to deal with a mother

185

who decides in the middle of the night to take a walk and the walk lasts three months. I'm not the greatest kid in the world, but I know enough to know she's not fit to raise me. I was thinking about that when we were climbing up the side of the mountain yesterday. I kept thinking how strong I am and how I'm not such a bad person after all. No matter how much I thought about it, though, I couldn't make my mother out to be a good person. I don't think good people just walk out on their kids and don't even give a thought as to whether or not the kids are going to eat. I used to think that maybe she did it because I had done something wrong. I know better now. She does it because she's got a whole bunch of problems herself. She had those problems long before I was born. I don't care if no one guarantees me anything, I want to go to a foster home. At least I might stand a chance. I don't stand any chance at all with my crazy mother."

"The counselors told me that they thought if my whole family got some help that I'd probably be better off staying with them." Marsha sounded sad about the decision her caseworker had made. "It's almost like I envy you guys. I'm outright jealous of Cory. She's really the only lucky one here. She's got both her parents and her home is okay. You are lucky, Cory. Do you know that?"

Until Cory had come to Springdale she had no idea how difficult it was for some youngsters her age to survive. Even so, it was still hard for her to agree. "If I'm so lucky, why don't I trust them? Why don't I feel good about myself?"

Lester counseled her. "I think you feel better about yourself now than before you came out here. Or, am I wrong?"

"Sure I'm proud of some of the things I've done" Cory smiled. "I never even thought I could walk this much let alone do it with a pack on my back. I'm most proud of just doing without water! My God! I didn't think I could get through the day without four sodas!" Cory looked around at all of them. "I feel like I belong. I've never felt that way before." Cory dropped her head as she didn't want them to see her sadness. "I don't want to be the way I am. I want to be like other kids."

Charley nodded to Marsha. She knew what he wanted her to do. Marsha reached over and put her arm around Cory. "It's okay, Cory. We all want to be normal." Then Marsha broke down and cried. "Boy, I'm some help. I'm as bad as Cory."

They all sat in silence for a moment. Then Charley said, "You guys keep talking about wanting to be normal. Who's to say what normal is. You don't have any way of knowing what kind of problems other kids your age are hiding. It so happens that with all of you, your problems hit the surface. Maybe that's better because you can get some help. Don't make yourselves sound like you're crazy. What you're feeling *is* normal. Just about everyone wants to belong. Even cows move around in herds. You all need to quit beating yourselves over the head and finding fault with who you are. If you could just get it straight that beating up on people or trashing a store or stealing are not going to make the problems go away. That kind of stuff only adds to the problems.

"And I might add," Charley shoved the heel of his boot back and forth through the pine needles on the ground, "you're not all going to find that foster homes are the answer. There aren't enough of them to go around. About the last thing most people want is another teenager in their home. There's a good chance some of you are going to go to a group home. There's also a good chance some of you might not be given that choice, either. You might end up having to learn how to survive within your home even if it's a rotten home."

"I'm not going back." Ginger hit her fist on the ground. "No matter what, I'm not going back with my father."

"Me neither," Marsha agreed. "I'll never go back and let that stepfather of mine hurt me or my sister. Springdale better find some other answer for me, or I'm running away to California."

"You don't even know where California is," Winnie challenged. "I hear all these kids say they're going to run away to California. What's in California is what I'd like to know?"

Sean smiled. "It's warm. They think they won't need any winter coats. When I'm on the streets, the last thing I want to be doing is carrying a heavy coat."

"Do you get lonely out on the streets?" Gene asked.

188

"Sure. There are all kinds of people out there. None of them are part of my life. When you get right down to it, I work real hard at keeping most of them out of my life. There's some really weird ones out there. I think I'm more likely to make it if I stay away from them."

Charley's heart went out to the young man. There was nothing about Sean that wasn't decent. If ever a boy deserved a break, it was Sean. He hoped more than anything that Sean would be one of those fortunate enough to be placed in a foster home. Then Charley looked at the others. There really wasn't a one of them who didn't deserve a break and a better life. "I think we better be thinking about getting to sleep. It's been an interesting night and a lot of good things have been said, but we're going to need our sleep. Tomorrow is going to be one of our longest days."

Each of them stood up and said goodnight to one another. Lester waited next to Charley. "I want them all to make it."

"You mean tomorrow?"

"Not just tomorrow, but for the rest of their lives. I don't want any of them to end up like me and Rower."

Charley patted Lester on the back. "If we can give them some confidence in themselves, they just might make it."

"It takes some lucky breaks, too."

"Until we get back, Les, let's just worry about the confidence. Goodnight. See you bright and early."

CHAPTER TWELVE

Winnie handed out a mixture of cereal and dried bananas while Sean and Gene wrapped the ropes as they had been taught to do. The others stood looking in the direction of the mountain they would be climbing. They could see the crest that they had to reach before two in the afternoon.

Sean bent his elbow and wrapped the rope around his arm. "Looks pretty far away, doesn't it, Gene?"

"Do you think we'll make it?"

"We've made it so far."

Gene checked to make sure that the picks were placed next to the ropes. "Hey, Sean, do you think I've changed? I mean are any of you guys starting to like me?"

Sean laughed at Gene's quizzical look. "Yeah, Gene, you're mellowing out. We can all just about tolerate you."

"Listen, I'm for real. I know inside I just don't feel as ticked off as I used to be. I think it's all these trees or fresh air. What do you think?"

Sean stopped what he was doing to think about what Gene said. "You know, I can't figure out what it is. Here we all are out in this forest. These trees never seem to come to an end. I don't know how many times I felt like I was going to starve to death or fall off a cliff, and somehow I feel safer here than I've ever felt. I'd like to find a job out here and stay here for the rest of my life. I get so sick of those dirty streets. Everything seems clean here. I almost hate to go back."

"That's what I guess it is with me. You're not going to

laugh or anything if I tell you something."

"Why should I?" Sean looked very serious.

"I don't ever want to go back. I wish I could live out here. That's why I thought it was strange when you said you felt safe here. There ain't nobody ever going to bother us here. No old man belting down booze and screaming and yelling. Just birds making their noises. Hey, who'd have thought a guy like me would ever have thought about birds? I used to shoot them with an air rifle." Gene regretted what he said. "Don't tell anyone. I'd be ashamed if anyone found out."

"You can trust me, Gene." When Sean said the word *trust* he thought about Cory. "Can I tell you something, Gene? This is just between you and me. You got that."

"Got it." Gene liked it that Sean was going to share something very private with him. No one had ever done that.

"It's about Cory." For a moment Sean was sorry that he'd brought up the subject. "I'm nuts about her. I don't know why because I don't like a lot of the things she says. I just know that being around her does something to me."

"She's okay. She's not my type. Cory's always on a downer. I like girls who smile and laugh. Cory takes everything too seriously."

"Maybe that's why I like her. I hate silly girls."

"Well, you know how Cory's always saying she doesn't want to talk about her problems because she doesn't think she has any compared to the rest of us. She's right. I want

191

to crack her one when she starts in about what she thinks is a tough life. That girl doesn't know what a tough life is. She ought to try picking herself up from the bottom of the stairs after her old man has thrown her down them. Don't you get tired of listening to her gripe? Like what does she have to complain about?"

"We're all different, Gene." Sean was sorry he had mentioned how he felt about Cory. He didn't want to have to defend her. It never bothered Sean when Cory talked about her home life or the problems that she had at school. Sean simply liked hearing her talk. There was something about the way she cocked her head and squinted her eyes that made her look very appealing. "They're getting ready to pull out."

Sean and Gene picked up the ropes and picks and handed them to each one in the group. Charley led them through the forest as they climbed upward. Within an hour there were fewer trees and more rocks and boulders. The steep climb slowed them down as they made their way around or over the boulders. By lunch they were ready for a rest. No one talked very much as they once again ate the dried food that Winnie handed out. "Here's your hamburger, french fries, and soda. Just like you ordered."

Marsha took the food from Winnie. "Cut it out, Winnie. We're too tired for your stupidness."

"Loosen up, grouch. We got a long way to go." Winnie stared up at the crest that still looked so far off. "A long way."

192

By one o'clock it was obvious that they would make it to the crest by two. One by one they held on to the large chain that had been drilled into the mountain so that hikers could cross the narrow ledge. Not one of them showed any fear when they looked down at the drop off. Charley smiled at the progress they had made. It was only a few days ago that he had to talk most of them into crossing a far less dangerous path. As often happened, the group got their second wind and made it to the crest more quickly than they had made the climb earlier in the day.

"What happened to all the trees?" Ginger looked around at the rocks and low-growing shrubs.

"It's too cold and windy up here," Lester answered. "We crossed the timberline a while back."

"What's a timberline?" Winnie asked.

It still amused Lester that years ago all he knew were city streets. Now he knew the names of trees and flowers. "That's the point at which trees don't grow. Look at those little flowers over there, Winnie. Tiny as they are, they come right up through the rocks. Says a lot about nature."

Winnie bent over to look at the small purple flowers that poked through solid rock. "How come flowers can grow through rocks?"

"Hardy, man. Just plain hardy. That's what you got to get like. Get like those flowers, boy, and you'll make it."

The canteens were passed around and all of them took a drink. There wasn't a one of them who didn't want more than the few swallows they were allowed. Rower gathered up the canteens after each of them had their drink. "I probably shouldn't tell you this, but once we get down the side and across the river, you can have all the water you want."

A loud cheer echoed through the mountains. Then they picked up their gear and walked to the point where they were to begin repelling down the side of the mountain.

"Oh, God." Marsha put her hand to her chest. "Why does it look so much farther down than it looked when we were coming up?"

Charley warned. "Don't think about going all the way down. You just have to make it to that ledge." Charley pointed to a wide shelf that was about twenty feet below them. "Just remember what we've taught you and what you've practiced." He wrapped the rope around his waist and secured it where the others stood. "You do your part, and I'll do mine. See you on the ledge." Charley dropped over the side, pushing his thick boots against the hard rock. As his body moved out away from the mountain, those at the top let the rope drop to lower Charley closer and closer to the ledge. In no time at all, Charley waved from the shelf. "Next."

One by one they dropped over the side and repelled themselves to the waiting arms below. Marsha was the only one whose timing was off. Her feet did not push her away from the rock soon enough. Her knuckles scraped against the rock and she called out, "Oh, that hurt. My hand hurts so much."

Rower called down. "You're going to have to forget the hurt, Marsha. Push off with your feet. Then push again. You got to get your body moving."

The others yelled encouragement. Sean screamed out, "Hey, Marsha, if you can use the bushes as a toilet, you can do this. This is a lot easier than a bowel movement."

They looked up and watched her shove her feet against the side of the drop off. Soon her body was sailing out away from the rock and Lester lowered her down a few more feet. "You're doing great, girl. Just keep going."

When Marsha's feet landed on the ledge, she breathed a sigh of relief. "I came down because I didn't have any place else to go. My hand still hurts. Look." She held up her hand. The knuckles were cut and bleeding.

Charley took some water from the canteen and dripped it across the knuckles. Then he wrapped a scarf around the injured hand. "You going to be able to make it?"

"You're darn right I am," Marsha grinned. "No one is leaving me behind." Marsha grabbed Cory's arm. "I'm so proud of myself. I just think I'm about the neatest person who ever lived."

"You did great, Marsha." Cory clasped Marsha's arm. "We're all doing great. How did we all get so great?"

Charley smiled at them. "You might not realize it, but coming down that mountain didn't make you great. You were the same person at the top that you were at the bottom. You just didn't realize when we started out six days ago that you were great. Something had to make you aware of it. It just so happens it was the side of a mountain. Come on. We've got a fair distance to go."

Sean wrapped the ropes around his arm. "Notice how he said *fair* distance instead of a *long way*. That's the best news I've heard today."

They wound their way down what almost looked like a path. Each followed the advice of Charley and found a thick branch to aid them in walking. When Cindy asked why her legs hurt after days of walking, Charley explained that she was using a different set of muscles going down the mountain than she had used going up. Cindy did no more than shrug her shoulders and comment that by tomorrow her legs would be used to it.

The sound of the river could be heard long before they reached the water. Cory thought back to how afraid she had been when she first heard the roar of the water and she ran into the woods. Now the gushing water signalled that the worst part of the descent was over. They had to cross the river and then they would be heading back toward the forested area and easier traveling.

The narrow river waters rushed at the rocks and boulders that lay between where they stood and the side to which they had to get. As the water moved along it formed white foam. Gene put his hand in the water. "That's pretty cold."

"Looks wicked." Winnie stared at the water dropping out of the mountain and racing downward. "I don't know why, but that water scares me more than the drop-offs in the mountains."

Ginger stood back a little. "I just keep telling myself I never came down a mountain before and I made it. I never crossed a river before, but I know I'll make it."

"That's what we want to hear." Charley again handed out the canteens. "All that water is so close and we have to sip our water. You can't trust the river water anymore. No telling what's in it. Get yourselves a drink while we wait on Lester."

Lester had pulled up the rope after the last one had dropped to the ledge below. Then he made his way down a steeper slope, but one which could be reached on foot. Almost as Charley had spoken his name, Lester appeared on the other side of the river. "Made it." He waved to them. Then Lester stepped across some rocks and entered the river. He wrapped his arm around a tree. "Ready."

Charley entered the water first. He held on to one end of the rope while Sean held the other. "It's going to jerk some when that water hits me. Hold tight. You're all going to feel like the water is going to drag you along, but we got you. Just keep moving. No matter what, don't let go of the rope."

They watched Charley make his way across to the other side. Several times his feet went out from under him as the force of the current knocked him down. As he neared the other side, Lester reached out and grabbed him. "One down. Nine to go."

Cindy screamed out, "I'm scared." Then she held

tightly to the rope and tried to make her way to the other side. She could feel a piece of her tooth chip off as she clamped her mouth tightly closed. "Please. Please. Get me to the other side." Water washed over her head and she gasped for air just as Charley put his arm out and pulled her across the rocks to the other side.

"That a girl. Next." Charley made it look as if it were easy. Every time he brought a group out, though, his pulse pounded when he thought it was always possible that one of them could be injured.

Jeff gave a deep sigh and plunged into the water. He realized he had made a mistake when he went in head first. It took him several seconds to right himself so that his head was above the water. A grin spread across his face and it remained there until he was pulled ashore and collapsed next to Cindy. "I'm not doing that ever again."

"Be quiet or they'll hear you and get scared." Cindy removed her shoes and stockings. "That's the most frightening thing I've ever done in my life. I could feel that water pulling me with all its might. I thought for sure I was a goner."

"I nearly was." Jeff lay on his stomach. "I don't even want to watch them."

Cory carefully moved to the edge of the rocks that stuck out of the water. She turned to Sean. "Why do I suddenly not feel so great?"

"They made it and you will, too. Think positively." His gut feeling was that something was going to happen.

Sean almost wanted to grab her to keep her from taking the first step. Her face looked pale and frightened. Cory reached the half-way point and stepped up on a rock instead of staying in the water as Charley had told them to do.

"Get off the rock, Cory," Charley yelled across the water. "The force of the current will knock your legs out from under you."

A look of panic crossed Cory's face as she felt the pressure of the water bend her knees. Instead of toppling toward Charley, she fell over backwards and let go of the rope.

Charley cursed. Again and again he had warned them all not to ever let go of the rope no matter what happened. He saw Cory being carried along on her back. The current was carrying her downstream and away from the side where Charley could get to her.

"Grab the tree, Cory." Sean raced along the shore. He was only a few feet from her, but the current was carrying Cory faster than Sean could run. "Turn on your stomach and grab the tree and hold on." Sean knew that if Cory could turn herself around and hold on to the limb hanging over the river, he could get to her and pull her out. Sean looked back and saw Rower and Gene coming up behind him. Rower carried a rope. He held it up so that Sean could see it.

From the other side of the river Charley kept pace with them. "Don't get in the water until they can throw you the rope. Don't double our problem. Do you hear me, Sean?

You'll need help." Charley never lost sight of Cory. All the color had drained from her face. "They're coming, Cory. There's the limb. Get it. Hold on to that limb. If it kills you, Cory, hold on." Charley was glad that it was Sean who would reach her first. If anyone would do the right thing, it would be Sean.

Cory reached up as she passed under the limb. Her right hand caught hold first. Then her left hand crossed over and she took hold of the limb with both hands. Sean saw the terror in her face. More than anything he wanted to step into the water and move toward her. To do that was to take a chance that he too might be pulled downstream. Others would have to risk their lives to save him. "In a second, Cory. In just a second Rower will be here." As he said the words, Rower threw him the rope. Sean quickly tied it around his waist and waded out into the stream. His hands barely touched Cory's. "Drop, Cory. I got you."

Cory looked down at the foaming water that raced past her. She could not turn loose of the limb even though her hands and arms ached from holding on. "Can you catch me?" Those were the first words that Cory had spoken since she had toppled in the river.

"Trust me, Cory. I'll get you." Sean screamed above the roar of the water. "I won't let anything happen." Sean moved closer to the deep water where Cory desperately clung to the branch. "Now, Cory. Let go now."

Cory's eyes met his for only a second. Then she turned loose of the branch. She felt herself go under the water before Sean grabbed her arm and pulled her toward him. "You're safe. You're okay now, Cory. We got you." The whitecaps slapped at their faces as Rower pulled them both toward him.

"Man, what a day." Rower reached down for Cory's hand. "You okay, girl?"

She managed a nod. As she sat down on the edge of the river she felt weak and nervous. "How will I ever get across?" It suddenly struck her that today was like the night in the woods when they made her do what she most feared doing. "You're going to make me go across. I know it."

"Charley," Rower yelled to their leader. "What we going to do?" Rower did not want the responsibility of making the decision that would put Cory back in the river.

"Let her rest for a few minutes." Charley walked back up to the point from which the rest of them would have to start. Those who remained on the other side were nervous. Watching Cory struggle to keep from being carried down the river or drowning had unnerved them all. To get Jeff and Cindy back to the other side and then to return back down the trail would take too much time. They'd run out of food and water before they got back. "We have to go on. There's no turning back. You know that, Rower."

Cory took Sean's hands. "You saved me."

"It could have been any one of us. I just happen to run faster than the rest of them."

"I've got to go across. I know that. It scares me."

"I expect so." Sean helped her up. "I'm scared myself."

Just looking at Cory made Rower nervous. "We can send some of the gear across for now. Maybe you need to take it easy for a bit, Cory." He couldn't get the picture of her frightened face out of his mind.

"If I don't go right now, I'll never do it." Cory was close to tears.

"I'll go with her." Sean volunteered. "We can tie ourselves together and cross. Okay, Cory. I'll be with you."

Cory shook her head. "No one else went across with someone holding on. I'm going to make it on my own." She squeezed Sean's arm. "I had to trust you when I was hanging onto the limb. I had to believe that you'd get me and pull me back. When I hit the water I felt relief because I touched your hand and felt you carrying me along. If I could trust you, I can trust myself. I'm going to do it on my own." Cory stepped to the edge of the water. "You ready, Charley? You ready because here I come." Cory held tightly to the rope that still dangled in the water. The force of the current struck her legs and she let them float out from beneath her as Charley pulled her along toward the other side. White caps struck her in the face several times, but each time she came to the surface and moved closer to where Cindy and Jeff stood waiting.

Jeff reached out to her. "You're something else, Cory. I sure couldn't have gone back in if that had happened to me. I swear you got guts."

Cory heard the clapping from the side where Sean and the others stood. Cory's breath came in deep gasps. "I'm like Marsha," she smiled. "I guess I am something else, Jeff. Someone pretty special."

Charley walked over and hugged her. "You've always been someone special, Cory. It's a darn shame you nearly had to drown to prove it to yourself."

CHAPTER THIRTEEN

Martin sat down opposite Mrs. Knight. Cory lowered herself into the chair next to Martin. Today would be her final review. What was said and done at this meeting would determine whether or not she went home. Cory watched Mrs. Knight reading the summary that Martin had given her.

"It looks good, Cory. Martin thinks that you're ready to go home."

A part of Cory hoped that they would think she wasn't ready to go home. After nine months at Springdale, Cory felt more comfortable at the detention center than she did at home. "I think I'm okay now."

Martin frowned. "Is that the most you can say for yourself?"

"I don't know what else to say. Do you want me to brag about myself?"

Mrs. Knight smiled. "That wouldn't be a bad idea. What can you tell me about yourself, Cory, that would make me believe you're not going to end up back here or in some other facility? Convince me that you're a good risk." Mrs. Knight felt that Cory was among those who stood the best chance of not getting in trouble again simply because she had parents who were concerned about her.

"I think I've overcome my biggest problem."

"What do you think your biggest problem was?" Martin tapped his pencil and looked directly at the young girl.

"I couldn't trust anyone. Now I understand that..."

Cory looked confused. She dropped her head. "I guess I don't know how to explain what happened to me. I just know I feel differently now about my parents. They didn't mean to lie to me. I suppose they just couldn't live together. It had nothing to do with me. It was just them."

"Have you told your mother and father how you feel?" Mrs. Knight wanted to know more about what Cory was thinking. "It's important that you get all this out in the open. If you don't, you're going to go on resenting them. It's not good to hold grudges."

Cory shook her head. "I don't hold any grudges. I can see how my mother was trying. She loved me, but she just didn't know what to do with me. I still think my dad has stronger feelings toward Rory than he has toward me. I've got to do something about how I feel toward Rory."

"Would you say that you're jealous of Rory?" Martin asked.

"He never does anything wrong, and here I end up in a detention center."

Mrs. Knight closed Cory's folder. "Rory is only two years old. Two-year-olds are a lot easier to deal with than teenagers. Your father reacts to what the boy does, and probably most of what the child does is cute. You're at an age where just about everything you do looks like a full-scale rebellion. You can't compare yourself to a toddler because you'll lose out every time."

"He's awfully cute." Cory bit her lip and tried to keep from crying. "I'm just pretty ordinary looking."

"You're beating yourself over the head, Cory, and you don't have to do that." Martin reached over and took Cory's hand. "We've worked on this a lot in group. Not many of us see ourselves as others see us. There's nothing the matter with the way you look, but I can't convince you of that. You have to convince yourself just as you convinced yourself that you could trust others. There's only so much that others can do for us. Then something inside us has to take over and we have to help ourselves. Once you leave here, you darn well have to be ready to help yourself."

"Let's talk a minute about school, Cory." Mrs. Knight interrupted Martin. "How do you see that situation?"

"I don't know what you mean." Cory really did not understand what Mrs. Knight wanted her to say.

"You were a loner at school. School can be tough enough when things are going right. It's worse when you feel left out. You could easily drift in with the wrong crowd again."

"No," Cory shook her head. "I'd never get in again with Matt or anyone like him. He never cared about me. Matt and Nicole just used me." Cory glanced up at Mrs. Knight. "Now I sound paranoid. I don't mean it that way. It's like my parents really care about me. I know that now. I was acting weird about my parents, but I don't think I'm weird when it comes to Matt. He couldn't have cared about me or he wouldn't have asked me to do some of that stuff. You don't ask someone you love to steal. That's what I mean. Then Matt and Nicole didn't even try to help me. I just quit caring about anything. That's why I got in even more trouble. That's not going to happen again no matter how alone I feel at school."

Mrs. Knight smiled at Cory. "I think you're getting to the point where your head is screwed on right. Are you going to have any problem with our talking to your counselor at school?"

"Do you mean do I care if she knows about me being here?"

"She already knows that. It might be, though, that we can make some suggestions on how she can help you." Mrs. Knight looked very serious. "It's not going to be easy, Cory."

"I'm not afraid. I think I can make it okay."

Martin sighed. "Oh, for the hardy, blind courage of the young." He stood up and pushed his chair back in place. "You ready to go say your goodbyes before we pull out of here?"

Cory reached out and shook Mrs. Knight's hand. "Thank you, Mrs. Knight, for helping me. I think I learned a lot here. Maybe you're not going to believe this, but I'm going to miss Springdale. The best friends I ever had are here."

"I believe you, Cory. I've seen it with others. Don't forget I've been in this business for a long time. There are a lot of young people who finally learn at Springdale how to make friends."

Cory walked down the hall toward the building where her dorm was located. As she watched some of the teams playing volleyball it reminded her of the first day when she arrived at Springdale. Cindy waved to Cory. Cory waved back, and thought that Cindy was among the lucky ones. She would stay at Springdale until a group home could be found for her. Ginger and Marsha, like all the boys on Cory's team, would be returned to their families. Mrs. Knight had fumed and demanded of the courts that something better be done for the youngsters who would be leaving Springdale in time for the beginning of the fall semester. No foster homes could be found and there was no space at any of the group homes. Within three days of the time that Sean was to be released, Charley showed up at Springdale to let Mrs. Knight know about a program to which Sean could be sent. In addition to having the boys complete high school, they were trained to fight forest fires. For Sean it meant leaving the state and saying goodbye to his family and to Cory.

Saying goodbye to Sean was one of the hardest things that Cory ever had to do. When they found out that Sean would be released to his parents, Cory and Sean made plans to meet once a week. Cory was sure that if she could go on seeing Sean, she would not feel so isolated and alone. Sean had assured Cory that no matter what went wrong in school, he would see her on the weekend and somehow make it up to her for anything that had gone wrong during the week. Knowing that he would be there to support her and to help her made going home seem easier. When she found out about his going to another state, she was overwhelmed with sadness.

"Just tell me that you don't want me to go, and I won't do it, Cory." As much as he cared about Cory, he hoped that she wouldn't ask him to stay.

"You have to go, Sean. It's about one of the luckiest breaks you could get. I can only imagine what would happen to you if you had to keep wandering around the streets. It could be months before your parents get jobs and get themselves back on their feet. You got to do what's best for you. I think it would be exciting learning how to fight forest fires."

"We can write." Sean took Cory's hands. "I know it won't be the same like seeing each other, but at least we'll know what the other one is doing. They told me I'll get leave. Like in the army or something. I can come back and see you."

"Maybe you could even spend Christmas at our apartment." Cory smiled thinking about how much Sean would add to her life if she could look forward to seeing him over the holidays. "We live in a pretty small place, but I know my mom would make room for you. I've told her all about you." Cory thought about how much she had shared with her mother on the last few visits home. Cory never wanted her mother to know anything about Matt. With Sean things were different. She wanted her mother to know everything about him.

Cory sat down with Sean to wait for the van that would take him away. He scraped his foot back and forth along the edge of the grass. "Seems like we're always waiting for that darn van to take us some place or to bring us back."

"Not anymore." Cory looked sadly at Sean. "This will be your last time. In a few days it will be my last time. Do you think we'll get in trouble for this?" Cory referred to the rule at Springdale that forbid boys and girls from being alone with each other.

"If I'm not mistaken, that's old Martin behind the blinds. He's been peeking out at us since we got here. He's not a bad guy. I'd think he gets fed up messing around with kids like us."

"He helped me, I know that. Martin, the tree limb, and you." Cory squeezed his hand. "Do you think we love each other, Sean?"

"I guess so. I know I care what happens to you."

"But you care about Cindy and Jeff and all the others."

"It's different with you, though, Cory. I mean I *really* care."

"Are there girls at that place where you're going?"

"Why?" Sean grinned. "Are you jealous?"

"I suppose so."

"Naw. Just guys like me. I know there are going to be boys where you're going." Sean wanted to hold her hand, but he was sure that such a gesture would bring Martin out of the building.

"I won't go out with any of them." Cory shrugged her

shoulders. "As if they'd ask me out, anyhow."

"Sure they will. You're pretty."

"I am not," Cory denied.

"If they do ask you out, are you going to go?"

"No, Sean. You're the only one I'll ever care about. Even if you're hundreds of miles away, you'll still be the only one I'll ever care about."

On the day of her release Cory walked toward the dorm to get her things. She looked at the spot where she and Sean had sat and said their goodbyes. Only four days had passed and it already seemed to Cory as if Sean had been gone for months. She entered the dorm and picked up the few belongings that she had been able to keep at Springdale. Then she headed for the study hall where she knew Ginger would be. Cory opened the door and signaled to the teacher that she had a pass. The teacher looked at the piece of paper that authorized Cory to say goodbye to her friend.

"Just a minute, Cory." The teacher returned inside to let Ginger know that Cory was waiting in the hall.

Ginger came out and put her arms around Cory. "I can't believe you're leaving." Tears were already falling down her face. "What are we going to do without each other? You're the best friend I've ever had."

"You, too." Cory hugged her. "You'd think we'd all be happy to be leaving this place. I still feel just terrible from Sean leaving. Now I have to say goodbye to you."

"It's going to be different with us, though, Cory.

211

Sean's pretty far away. You and me are still going to get to see each other."

"Are you scared?"

"Sure I'm scared. I told Mrs. Knight that I'm not taking anything off my dad. She said I didn't have to. I got this phone number to call. Mrs. Knight said if he puts a hand on me, I'm to call this number and get him arrested. She told him that, too. I don't think he believed her, but I can guarantee that I'll get the cops to haul him right out of his own house. You wait and see."

"I believe you, Ginger. You don't have to take his hitting on you."

"Are you scared?"

"Not really. I guess I'm getting like you guys. I mean I'm starting to think how lucky I am compared to what all of you have to put up with. My mom and me are going to go to counseling. She's talked to my dad about some of the things that make me afraid. Mrs. Knight said that I still had to tell him myself, but at least he knows I'm not this really bad person." Cory laughed, "I'm like a lot of teenagers. I'm just sort of confused as to how things got to be the way they did."

"Isn't that the truth?" Ginger walked down the hall with Cory. "I wish we didn't live so far apart."

"It's not so far. You wait and see. We'll get to visit together a lot. I probably can come and stay with you and you can come and stay with me."

"You got to be kidding! Stay at my place. It's a dump

and my dad would insult you and call you names. He's nuts. Can you believe those counselors! They're going to try and teach me how to live with a nutty father. Maybe they'll find out how nuts he is and get me out."

"I hope so, Ginger. I really hope so." Cory stood at the top of the stairs and gave Ginger a hug. "I better get going. You got my phone number and all. Right."

"I'll call you just as soon as I get home. Jeff said he'd call us, too. Bye, Cory. I love you."

"I love you, too, Ginger." Cory blew Ginger a kiss. Then she ran down the stairs.

Martin stood near the door of the van. Four other youngsters were waiting to be taken back into town. "Got your goodbyes said?" Martin touched Cory's arm as she passed him.

"That's all I've been doing all week is saying goodbye." Cory wiped at the tears and boarded the van.

Martin walked around to the back of the van. "I know there's some pain in saying goodbye to this place. Believe me, though, if you get yourself in trouble, you won't be coming back to anything like Springdale. I can guarantee you that Springdale is one in a million. I've worked at some of the other places. The kids are knocking each other over to get out of the detention centers. You guys have been on a gravy train." Then he closed the doors, wondering if any of them believed the truth of his words.

Cory leaned back in her seat and watched the country disappearing behind her. It was hard to believe that nine months had passed since she had sat in the van that brought her to Springdale. Her mind rambled with all sorts of thoughts. Mostly, though, she thought about Sean. Cory imagined him as she had last seen him when he boarded the van. She looked toward the seat where the King boy now sat. That was the seat that Sean had taken just before the van pulled away from Springdale.

Martin turned the last corner that took the van behind the court buildings. A small group of youngsters stood close together by the door that led to the juvenile court-room. Cory looked at them and wondered if she had looked that frightened and that bewildered on the day that she was taken to Springdale. She stepped down and moved away from the van. A young girl caught Cory's eye. There was something about her that reminded Cory of herself. The girl stood away from the others. Her eyes darted around suspiciously as though there was a need to make sure that no one came near her.

Cory walked over to the girl. "My name is Cory. I've just come from Springdale. It will be all right, you know. It really will be. If you let them help you, you'll be okay."

She stared blankly at Cory. Then she pulled herself back up against the wall to put as much space as possible between her and Cory.

Margaret came rushing up to her daughter. "At last you're home for good." She wrapped her arms around Cory's shoulders. "Let's make it work this time. Okay?"

Cory linked her arm inside her mother's and smiled.

"Nothing is going to turn out perfect. I know that, Mom. But like you said, let's work on it." Cory turned around to look at the girl again. "Mom, who does that girl remind you of?"

"Which girl?"

"The one with the vacant look on her face. She's leaning up against the wall."

Margaret glanced over at the young girl. "No one that I know of. Does she remind you of anyone?"

"Yes. She reminds me of someone I used to know."

CHAPTER FOURTEEN

Cory no longer noticed many of the things that she once hated about the smallness and the drabness of the apartment where she and her mother lived. Cory could see, as her counselor pointed out, that the anger and hostility she felt toward her parents made everything seem worse than it was. Once Cory was able to talk to her parents about her fears, much of the anger disappeared. Her father now understood that Cory deeply resented his leaving and had worried constantly that Rory would get all his attention. When her father reassured Cory that he loved her as much as he loved his young son, Cory now believed him.

At first the efforts Cory made to get to know the little boy were forced and far from genuine. When Cory offered to take him to the nearby playground, his mother hesitated, not wanting him to be alone with his older stepsister. Even Rory pulled away from Cory, running back to his mother and holding on to her leg. Cory saw in them what she had lacked herself for such a long time: trust. Looking at the blond-haired boy holding tightly to his mother's leg made Cory realize how long it took to build up trust in another person.

Cory turned to her father. "It's okay, Dad. Rory doesn't trust me yet."

"Oh, it's not that, Cory." Her father attempted to make Cory feel more comfortable. "All kids that age cling to their mothers. He's just shy."

"When I get to know him better, he won't be so shy

around me." Cory smiled at her brother. "We're going to become friends, Rory. We'll do lots of things together." Cory looked at the child's mother. The expression on her face made it clear that she was very doubtful that the older girl and her own young child would ever be friends.

"It will take time, Cory." Her dad put his arm around her shoulder. "Look how long it took us to work things through. We have worked them through, haven't we?" Even he had his doubts after so many years of tension and quarreling with his daughter.

Cory gave her father a hug. "I don't blame you, Dad, for not believing me. I was pretty much of a jerk. Maybe I'm growing up." Cory poured herself a glass of tea and sat down. "What's so strange is you'd just think that everyone in the same family would trust each other because they are a family. It doesn't happen that way. That's kind of scary, isn't it?"

"I've always trusted you, Cory."

"Come on, Dad, get real. I don't think it happens that way. Parents always wonder what their kids are up to. You mean to tell me you never thought I might be lying to you or doing things I wasn't supposed to be doing?"

Her father grinned. "When you put it that way, I guess you're right. Most of us think back to some of the stuff we pulled when we were teenagers. Now that *really* is a scary thought. We keep thinking what would happen if our kids did some of the things we did."

"Yeah, well, most of us do lie to our parents at one time

or another, and you guys lie to us. Does Rory ever lie?"

"Rory can't say enough words to make up a lie, but he tries to cover it up when he breaks something." He turned to Rory and held out his arms. "Don't you, little guy?" Rory came over and sat in his father's lap. "Right now, though, I guess he's too young to even think we might not be doing the right thing for him. When you get to be your age, you're not so sure. Do you think I'm trying to do the right thing for you, Cory?"

"I think so. I don't know that I always agree with you, and I sure don't like some of the things that you and mom do, but I guess I believe now that you both are doing the best you can. Oh, Dad, you wouldn't believe what some of the kids at Springdale have been through. It's sure not fair. My friend Ginger has had the police out to her house so many times since she left Springdale. I just wish they'd put her father in jail and get it over with. Then maybe Ginger could go some place else and live."

"There are a lot of people who have a rough way to go. It's a darn shame when it has to start so early for some of these kids."

"Like me?" Cory smiled. "I'm kidding, Dad. Just kidding."

Her conversation with her father was like many of the conversations she had with both her parents over the last few months. Cory had almost gone in the opposite direction of the way she had been. Instead of showing anger and hostility, her parents saw only a cheerful and forgiving daughter. No matter what her mother and father did, Cory said she understood and approved of what they had done or what they were doing. It was Mrs. Valdez, Cory's counselor at school, who first noticed that Cory was making too much of an effort to bury the past and to pretend it had never existed. It also bothered Mrs. Valdez that Cory's contact with other students had not improved any since last year. Cory still ate alone and walked to and from her classes by herself. Not once since Cory had returned to school did Mrs. Valdez ever see her with any other student.

When Cory entered the office of Mrs. Valdez, she was sure it was for the purpose of hearing how well she was doing. Cory was shocked when she found out that Mrs. Valdez was not pleased with what was happening to Cory. "Are things still going well at home?"

"Everything is wonderful."

"Wonderful, huh? What would you say if I told you I didn't believe your life is as wonderful as you say it is?"

Cory frowned. "Well, you asked me, and I told you."

Mrs. Valdez swiveled back and forth in her chair. "You know, Cory, when I was a kid my parents made me clean my plate. If I so much as left a crumb on the plate, I'd have to hear about the starving kids in Africa or Asia. Knowing that children were starving in other places didn't make me like asparagus any better."

A quizzical look crossed Cory's face. She did not understand the point Mrs. Valdez was trying to make. "I don't get it."

"Tell me again about some of the kids at Springdale."

"You mean where they went? What is it you want me to tell you?"

"How rough they had it."

"Why do you want me to do that?"

"Because you keep wanting to talk about them. You talk about them with me, and I know from what you said that you talk about them with your parents. What it amounts to, Cory, is that you believe you don't have a right to talk about your problems because your life isn't nearly as bad as their lives. You're probably right. Those young people are going through hell, but that doesn't mean you don't have a right to express your fears or your concerns."

"Compared to them, my life is a dream."

"And compared to the children in Africa and Asia, I had plenty of asparagus. Cory, you learned a lot at Springdale. I can just tell in talking with you that you did a great deal of growing up while you were there, but Springdale didn't create magic. Every time you come in here and I try to get you to open up, you tell me how great things are. You smile. You laugh. And you say that school is great and life at home is wonderful. Yet, when I see you in the halls, you are by yourself. In study hall you stare off into space. In gym you hold back and look like you hope someone is going to pick you for a team."

Mrs. Valdez stood up and came around to sit beside Cory. "Cory, you have to understand that you can't pretend life is beautiful when it's not. It's correct that your parents aren't drunks, and it's true that they don't beat you, and you don't have to deal with adults who are abusing you. I think that every time you want to complain about something or to express your fears, you think about your friends from Springdale. Your life seems so much better than what they face that you just keep quiet. I know for a fact, you're hurting. I recognize the look. Now do you want to lay it all out to me, or do I have to keep trying to drag it out of you?"

Cory felt trapped. She knew Mrs. Valdez was right, but to admit the truth meant to admit that she had been living a lie. "Things are better at home. I can talk to my parents about plenty of things now."

"Can you talk to them about school?"

"What about school? I'm passing everything."

"Sure you are. You're doing a hundred times better in your classes than you did last year. What I mean, though, is can you talk to your parents about feeling isolated and alone and about not belonging?" Mrs. Valdez blurted out what she felt was the bitter truth as she saw it.

Cory folded her hands together to keep them from shaking. "Why do you say that?" Cory was angry as she challenged Mrs. Valdez. "I don't care what these stupid kids think. I don't care that they don't talk to me."

"I think you do. It has to be hard. There's nothing wrong with wanting to belong. You found that out at Springdale. You know, Cory, your face lights up when you talk about Sean or Cindy or Ginger. They were important

221

to you, but they are not part of your daily life anymore. You need friends here at school. Everyone needs friends."

Cory looked up at the ceiling to avoid the direct stare of Mrs. Valdez. "So what am I supposed to do? They all just walk past me. They all know I was arrested and put away and they stare at me and talk about me. No one but the bums and crazy gang members even bothered to speak to me. I don't want anything to do with them because I'll just get in trouble again. You know, Mrs. Valdez, I can't make anyone talk to me."

"Have you tried talking to other students? Have you tried joining anything?"

"Why should I? They'll just ignore me. Besides, what would I join?"

"You can't assume other students won't talk to you until they actually *do* walk away from you, and as for joining something, this school has about twenty different clubs and organizations. Sign up for the thing that interests you."

Cory let out a deep sign. "You make it all sound so easy. It's not. Every time I sit down in the cafeteria, I'm sure the other kids are going to get up and leave me sitting there by myself. Then I have to sit there and listen to them making all their plans about where they're going and what they're going to do." Cory took a deep breath as her voice began to tremble. "If they just knew what it was like they'd be nice. Believe me, Mrs. Valdez, they just don't know what it's like."

"Maybe you ought to tell them." Mrs. Valdez stroked Cory's hair. "I guess there's some sort of irony to the fact that teenagers are so terribly sensitive about their own feelings, and then they don't always see how they are hurting someone else. That's life, though, Cory. You have to deal with life as it is. I'd really like for you to try. Just a few times. If it doesn't work, we'll talk about it again. But you have to quit pretending."

"It isn't all pretending," Cory defended herself. "I really am getting along better with my mother. I don't mind helping her. I do my share of the housework and we talk about lots of things. I see my dad more often, and I really am trying to get Rory to like me." Cory wrinkled her brows. "I just don't know about my stepmother. She's still not very friendly."

"I'm not saying things aren't better. I already told you that I'm pleased with the way things are going for you in your classes. I believe you when you say that you and your parents have come to some understanding. That's two areas that have improved. But you have two more years of school. You need to develop some friendships. Will you try, Cory?"

"It's hard."

"Am I saying it isn't hard? I'm just saying you have to try." Mrs. Valdez thought for a moment. She wanted to make sure that this was the right time to mention to Cory that she had spoken to Mr. Talbott, the English teacher. "I took it upon myself to intervene, Cory. I thought maybe

223

you could use a little help. I spoke to Mr. Talbott."

"Mr. Talbott." Cory thought about the tall, thin teacher who always seemed ready to explode with excitement. "I don't even have any of his classes."

"Mr. Talbott puts on the school plays. I told him that I thought you might try out for a part."

"Me! Try out for a part in a play! I'd die before I'd do that. I really would die before I'd get up in front of all the kids at school."

"I promise you, Cory, if you die, I'll come to your funeral. I want you to promise me that you'll summon up all your courage and show up at three o'clock in the assembly. He's expecting you."

"I couldn't do it."

"You just start thinking about all the things that you thought you couldn't do and that you've since done. Then you can try telling me that you can't do it. You could have just as easily fallen in with the wrong bunch here at school. You didn't do that. It took courage to stay away from those who would have befriended you for the wrong reasons. They would have been the wrong kind of friends, and you had sense enough to know that. I think there's more to you, Cory, than you give yourself credit for. Will you at least go to the assembly at three?"

The last thing Cory wanted to do was to comply with the request of Mrs. Valdez. Usually her last class of the day seemed to last forever. Today the time passed all too quickly. All the students filed out of the room and then dashed down the hall. Cory wandered slowly toward the assembly hall on the first floor of the building. Four times she opened the door, only to close it when she saw Mr. Talbott standing up on the stage arranging chairs. Finally when Cory heard him speaking to the other students, she knew she was going to have to go inside and take her place among those who had entered the assembly while she stood outside.

The students who sat in the first two rows turned to look when Cory walked down the aisle. Mr. Talbott smiled at her. "Good afternoon, Cory." He didn't know much about Cory. Mrs. Valdez had merely said that the girl needed help, and if anyone could help her, Mr. Talbott could. "Nothing important has happened yet, so you haven't missed much." He handed out the script for the play. "I want you each to find a partner. Then spend some time reading this script. You and your partner are going to act out part of the play. It will give you some practice with dialogue. Tomorrow you'll get a chance to step on stage and read your parts. What you'll find is that each of you will bring part of yourself to the role. Not any of you are going to read the dialogue in exactly the same way. Now get a partner, please."

Cory looked up and saw the face of a young man. "I'm Kevin. Kevin Gordon. You want to be my partner?"

As much as she tried, Cory couldn't return his smile. "I'm Cory." Her hands trembled when she realized that Kevin was the first person to introduce himself since she had returned to school.

"Are you nervous?" He moved toward the back of the assembly to get away from the others who were seeking places where they could practice the dialogue.

"Very much. I didn't want to do this. My counselor thought it would be good for me."

"I've always wanted to get into acting. My parents sort of fought me on this. Hey, I tell you my dad thought it was sissy stuff. If it didn't have to do with sports, he didn't want to hear about it. I finally convinced him I was going to try out this year for the plays. I hate arguing with my parents, but I had to make them believe this was the right thing for me." Kevin sat down. Then he quickly stood up. "Do you want to sit down or stand up?"

"Let's sit down and read through it a couple of times. Wait a minute," Cory smiled. "I don't even know what I'm talking about. I don't have the slightest idea what we're supposed to do. Do you usually sit down or stand up?" She noticed his eyes were quite blue.

"Let's sit down and read it through. Then we can stand up and say it because that's what we're going to have to do on stage."

Cory put it out of her mind that tomorrow she would have to get up in front of the others and read the dialogue. She read through the first two pages of the script. The story was about a young woman who could not relate to other people because she could not trust them with her feelings. As Cory read through her part, she felt the same pain that the young woman must have felt.

"Want to take a crack at it?" Kevin put the script in his lap.

"So we stand up now?"

"I guess." Kevin held up the script so that he could read his part of the father who is questioning his daughter about the pain she feels at being cut off from the rest of the family.

Cory read the young woman's explanation of what it was like to feel alone. When she finished, Kevin sat down and looked at Cory in amazement. "You are really good. My lines sounded dumb, but when you read your lines, it sounded like you knew exactly what she was going through. I'll bet you anything that you're going to get the part. I just can't believe it. Have you acted before?"

For a few minutes Cory thought how many times she pretended to be someone she wasn't. With Matt she had pretended to be interested in all the terrible things that he wanted to do just so that she would feel as if she belonged to someone. For the last few months she had pretended with her family that everything in her life was perfect when it wasn't. When she answered Kevin, Cory said, "I've never done any acting, but I've sure done a lot of pretending."

Unlike yesterday that passed all too quickly, this day the time wouldn't pass fast enough. For the first time in months Cory felt like she had something to look forward to. It had been so long since she had felt excited that she had almost forgotten how nice the feeling was. She didn't wait outside the assembly as she had done yesterday. Instead she went right in and sat down with the others. Kevin was waiting for her. The other students nodded to her and Cory managed to smile back. Mr. Talbott came bounding down the aisle and waved to all of them. "It's going to be a good day."

There were so many times when Cory wouldn't have agreed with what he said. Today, though, she thought that it truly was going to be a good day. Last night she had talked to Margaret about the play and about her partner. For the first time she admitted to her mother that it had been difficult to return to school and that it bothered her that none of the other students talked to her. Cory had hopes that maybe things could be turned around if she did as Mrs. Valdez suggested.

Mr. Talbott asked each of the partners to introduce themselves and to tell the others a little about themselves. "It's nice to know who we all are."

Cory listened to those who went before her. Then she closed her eyes and recalled what it was like to climb the mountain and wade across the river. As dangerous and tiring as those days of survival were, they seemed easy compared to what she now had to do. When her time came to go up to the stage, she reached over and touched Kevin's arm. "Ready?"

"If you are, I am." Kevin sucked in a deep breath. "You want to go first."

Cory stepped to the front of the stage. "My name is Cory. I'm a junior." Her knees started to shake when she suddenly realized they were all looking at her. "I missed most of last year because I was at a detention center." She wasn't sure why she said what she did except she knew she wanted to be honest. Cory recalled how Martin had advised them all that if they were truthful about their lives, they wouldn't have to wait for someone to sneak up on them and tell what they should have told about themselves.

"I signed up because I think I'd like to learn how to act. I also signed up because I don't really know anyone at school, and I think this would be a good way to meet other students." Cory felt a great sense of relief after she had spoken. "I guess that's all I have to say about me." She stepped back and waited for Kevin to come forward.

Mr. Talbott smiled at Cory. He knew it took a great deal of courage to say what she did. He came down the aisle to the front of the stage and clapped for Cory. Kevin followed the example set by Mr. Talbott. Then the other students joined them. "Come forth to the center of the stage, Cory." Mr. Talbott beckoned to her. "When the audience shows their approval, you need to take a bow."

Cory covered her mouth with her hands and blushed. Kevin took her hand and led her to the front of the stage. "Take a bow like Mr. Talbott says."

The smile on Kevin's face pleased Cory. She bent over in a deep bow. "Thank you all for welcoming me." Then she and Kevin returned to their positions at the center of the stage and read their parts.

There was no doubt in Mr. Talbott's mind who would get the lead role in the play. "Beautiful job. Just beautiful."

Cory and Kevin came back to their seats. "You were even better today, Cory."

Cory looked around at the students who were smiling at her and who said how good she was. Cory thought about how many good things she would have to say in her next letter to Sean. She leaned over and whispered to Kevin, "You know how the young woman in the play says that she's reached a turning point?"

"Yeah. What about it?"

"I just wanted to tell you that there really are turning points in life."